DEAD ON T...

"Devil One, snap ninety!" the controller shouted tersely.

It was an impossible command, directing Doberman to take a turn he couldn't afford to make. Immediately, his instrument panel lit up like Broadway—a ground radar station was tracking him.

The controller's next transmission was overrun by a Wild Weasel—a modified F-4 Phantom tasked with taking out SAMs. The pilot's words flew by so fast that Doberman could only get the gist, but that was enough—a missile battery they'd thought was dead had come back to life.

Worse, Doberman thought, *it's about to launch.*

Suddenly, two black slivers arced out of the darkness, streaking toward his A-10A, giving him just enough time to think—

Correction—it's already launched . . .

Don't miss the other explosive novels in the HOGS series:

HOGS

GOING DEEP

HOG DOWN

FORT APACHE

SERIES

Berkley Books by James Ferro

HOGS

HOGS #4
SNAKE EATERS

JAMES FERRO

BERKLEY BOOKS, NEW YORK

HOGS: SNAKE EATERS

A Berkley Book / published by arrangement with
the author

PRINTING HISTORY
Berkley edition / January 2001

All rights reserved.
Copyright © 2001 by Jim DeFelice

Cover art by Gerber Studio
Cover design by Oysterpond Group

This book, or parts thereof, may not be reproduced in any form without permission.
For information address: The Berkley Publishing Group,
a division of Penguin Putnam Inc.,
375 Hudson Street, New York, New York 10014.

The Penguin Putnam Inc. World Wide Web site address is
http://www.penguinputnam.com

ISBN: 0-425-17815-3

BERKLEY®
Berkley Books are published by The Berkley Publishing Group,
a division of Penguin Putnam Inc.,
375 Hudson Street, New York, New York 10014.
BERKLEY and the "B" design
are trademarks belonging to Penguin Putnam Inc.

PRINTED IN THE UNITED STATES OF AMERICA

10 9 8 7 6 5 4 3 2 1

PROLOGUE

The chaplain had only just arrived in the Gulf. He was very new to the Army, but was a sensitive man and conscientious, convinced that God had sent him here to do some good.

But how? His first service was scheduled for this very afternoon, and he couldn't think of anything to say in his sermon, or at least nothing that would be inspiring. The men here were on the front line, the trip wire of the allied defense. At any second, Saddam's minions could appear over the next sand dune and overwhelm them. He needed something powerful to encourage and comfort them. But he could think of nothing.

Finally, the minister decided to seek inspiration from the desert itself. He walked out from the sandbags and strolled into the open sand, shading his eyes from the sun. He gazed across the undulating desert, trying to imagine what this land might have been like three or four thousand years before, when God had come among the Israelites and smote their enemies.

At that instant the ground trembled and the chaplain felt himself being thrown down by the force of a heavenly wind. He writhed in the dirt, certain that he was experiencing heavenly enlightenment.

Or worse.

Turning his eyes upward, he saw not an angel but a black-green monster, ugly and ferocious, breathing fire. It roared overhead, shaking the marrow of his bones.

It took the minister a moment to realize it was not an apparition, and then another moment to connect the monster to a briefing one of the soldiers had given him earlier. The sandbagged position was directly in a flight line used by some of the Allied Coalition fighter-bombers returning from missions north. The plane was an A-10A Warthog, heading for a nearby air base to reload for another sortie.

The minister felt more than a little embarrassed as he pulled himself from the ground. But then he realized that it had, after all, been a message—if not entirely divine, certainly a useful one.

"The Apocalypse. Revelations. Of course," he said, brushing the sand from his trousers as he ran back to write his sermon.

It was later said to be the best ever preached in Saudi Arabia.

PART ONE

IN THE MUD

1

Fear made him stand up. Fear cocked his arm and straightened his legs. Fear snapped his finger on the Beretta's trigger, once, twice. Fear was everything he was, everything he felt, everything he did.

The Iraqi soldier fell to the ground.

Lieutenant William "BJ" Dixon ran forward and grabbed the man's fallen Kalashnikov rifle. There were shouts and footsteps in the rock quarry behind the soldier he'd just killed. He squatted, assault gun in his hand. He leaned forward to kneel and waited.

Finally, a pistol and then an arm appeared around the corner. The gun fired two, three times, unaimed. One of the bullets ricocheted off the sheer rock next to Dixon, but he did not flinch. He was beyond flinching. He waited for a clear shot.

The hand drew back. Dixon waited. Finally a face, baffled, scared, poked out from behind the corner.

Dixon pressed the rifle against his side as he pushed the trigger.

In the instant between reflex and reaction, he realized it was his own fear he saw in the man's face. By rights, Dixon shouldn't be here in the middle of Iraq, closer to Baghdad than Riyadh. By rights, he should be lying dead on the next hillside where the Delta Force commando patrol he'd been working with as a ground controller had been ambushed and pinned down.

Two of the three bullets Dixon fired in the quick burst from the Russian-made automatic rifle struck the Iraqi, the first passing directly through the man's heart. Dixon jumped up and ran forward, throwing himself to the ground as he reached the body. Falling past the corner of the sheer rock wall, he fired in the direction the man had come from. Luck and surprise caught two more Iraqis cold, both barely three yards away. Bullets spewed from his gun until it clicked empty.

Dixon rolled upward, pushing his knee under him to spring along the rock wall toward the two bodies. There were no other Iraqis that he could see. He threw away his empty rifle and grabbed one that had fallen between the two men. As he took it, he looked into the face of one of the soldiers.

The man gasped for breath. Tears streamed down the sides of his face.

Dixon saw that the man wore a belt across his chest with extra clips for the Kalashnikov. He reached down, curled his fingers around the canvas strap, and yanked it free with an immense heave.

The man screamed. His chest and stomach blotted with a fresh splurge of blood. His yelp turned into a spew of vomit.

To shoot him now would be a great mercy.

Dixon hesitated.

Blood mixed with the vomit sputtering from the man's mouth. He moved his lips, trying to say something.

A few days ago Dixon was merely a pilot—a Hog driver. He'd never dealt with something like this; it simply hadn't existed for him. He had never looked so close at death.

But his past lay in the ruined smoke of a nearby storage bunker, a probable NBC—nuclear-bacterial-chemical—facility the Delta team had targeted for Dixon's A-10A unit, the 535th Tactical Fighter Squadron, the Devil's Hogs. Everything Dixon had done until now, from shooting down a helicopter early in the air war to rescuing a Spec Ops sergeant a few hours ago, no longer mattered.

Fear was all. Fear and survival. He had to get the hell out of here before more Iraqis came. He had to run, and now, if he was going to live. There was no time for mercy.

The lieutenant closed his eyes and took a few steps away. Then he cursed and went back to the man, forcing himself to look as he pressed the muzzle to the soft temple of the agonized Iraqi and took away his pain forever.

2

Captain John "Doberman" Glenon heaved himself over the side of the A-10A cockpit, balancing precariously on the narrow steps of the attack plane's crank-down ladder. Doberman considered himself, without doubt, the luckiest man in the Gulf. He had just managed an emergency landing on a scratch strip controlled by American Special Operations Forces nearly a hundred miles deep in the Iraqi desert. With less than a sneeze worth of fuel in the sump at the bottom of his tanks, he'd fought off a last-second mechanical problem and parked his Hog ten feet from the end of the dangerously short strip.

Until today, Doberman had never really believed in luck. Now he'd belly up to a Lotto machine, blow a year's pay, and consider it an investment. He felt like he'd just nailed the prom queen.

The desert sun boiled off some of his exhilaration as the soles of his feet scraped along the grit of the sand-swept runway. He was alive against all odds—but he was also deep inside enemy territory, on the ground, with no jet fuel and no chance of getting some anytime soon. The concrete life raft he stood on was protected by less than a dozen Delta Force troopers and a handful of combat engineers who were working feverishly to throw up some sort of defense.

And less than a half hour before, he'd seen the body of a fellow squadron member sprawled in a rock quarry he and his wingmate had targeted for destruction. Lieutenant William "BJ" Dixon had been a nugget with a knack for getting his butt into places where it didn't belong, but that had only made Doberman like him all the more.

"Hey, Dog Man!" Doberman's wingmate, Captain Thomas "Shotgun" O'Rourke, ambled over. Shotgun's burly body—some might call it fat, though not to his face—hung half out of his flightsuit. He had landed a few minutes ahead of Doberman, also nearly out of fuel. "Where you figure they got the coffee going?"

"What makes you think they got coffee?" said Doberman.

"Green Berets always have coffee," said Shotgun. "It's one of the requirements. Like being an NCO. They have special courses just to teach these guys how to make it under fire."

Doberman shielded his eyes against the sand and sun as he stared at Shotgun's round face. It was hard to tell sometimes whether his wingmate was kidding or not.

Odds were he wasn't. There were only two things Shotgun considered sacred—driving Hogs, and coffee. He was undoubtedly the only attack pilot in the entire Air Force who carried a thermos of joe into battle.

"You will find coffee in the second dugout beyond the cement foundation," said a voice behind them. "Though I would note that the use of the word 'coffee' stretches the definition beyond reasonable tolerance."

Doberman spun around. Only one person in the Gulf spoke like that—Captain Bristol Wong, a Pentagon intelligence analyst who'd had the misfortune of wandering into Devil Squadron's readyroom shortly after the air war began. He had been promptly shanghaied as the unit's resident expert on Russian-made air defenses. Despite his prissy nature, Wong was actually a man of considerable talents; he had performed a tandem high-altitude skydive early that morning, delivering a mechanic to the covert base.

A mechanic who happened to be another member of Devil Squadron, Technical Sergeant Rebecca "Becky" Rosen.

Female Technical Sergeant Rosen, whose presence here violated any number of regulations, military necessity or not. It was as boneheaded a move as any Doberman had ever heard of.

"Hey, Braniac, how was the parachutin'?" asked Shotgun, slapping Wong on the back so hard the creases momentarily disappeared from the captain's fatigues. But only momentarily. Wong had donned a set of Spec Ops chocolate-chip camo fatigues; they looked as if he'd just ironed them.

Wong carefully removed Shotgun's hand from his back. "The parachuting, Captain, was an elementary operation that could have been accomplished by any member of the

Special Forces command. Obviously, I was assigned because Colonel Klee decided he didn't want me at his base."

"Gee, you think?" asked Shotgun.

"As for your being angry with me, Captain Glenon, as I can tell by your red cheeks"—Wong nodded in Doberman's direction—"I would suggest that the emotion is misdirected. Colonel Klee gave a direct order; I merely carried it out."

"Dog ain't mad; he's just sunburned," said Shotgun.

"Klee's an ass," spit Doberman.

"Undoubtedly. Nonetheless, given the contingencies involved, his order appeared lawful," added Wong. "And thus I saw it as my duty to carry it out. A fortuitous event, in any case."

"How do you figure that?" asked Doberman.

"There is now a mechanic here to see after your planes, as well as the helicopters," said Wong.

Rosen was hardly an expert on helicopters—and the ones in question were Army aircraft, not Air Force. But before Doberman could say anything more, they were interrupted by a sunburned middle linebacker who turned out to be the captain in charge of the base.

"I'm Hawkins," said the captain, shoving his fat hand into Doberman's. "Welcome to Fort Apache."

Hawkins wore a generic camo uniform without markings of unit or rank, but the snap in his voice left no doubt that he was in charge. He'd been wounded—there was a thick wrap around his midsection and another on one of his legs, and his rolled-up sleeves revealed a series of scrapes and gashes covered with caked-up antibacterial ointment. But there was no hint from his manner, let alone his quick movements, that any of these injuries had affected him.

Doberman—at five-four, short even for a pilot—shook the Delta officer's hand and began walking with him to his command post, a makeshift bunker in the concrete ruins.

Fort Apache had been established by Hawkins and his team as a staging and command center for American and British Special Operations troops looking for Scuds farther north in Iraq. The concrete landing strip had been started as an air base some years before by the Iraqis, and then abandoned. Located about five miles from the nearest highway, the concrete strip was surrounded by scrubland and desert. Two AH-6 Little Birds—armed scout helicopters specially adapted to "black" missions—had been assigned to Hawkins's team, and were hidden beneath desert-colored tarps just off the concrete.

The original plan had called for Hawkins's team to capture the strip and lengthen it to at least two thousand feet. That would make it long enough for emergency landings—and takeoffs—by stricken allied craft heavier than the Hogs. It would also allow a four-engined C-130 to land—actually, an MC-130, the Spec Ops chariot of choice. A specially modified model equipped with an airborne cannon as well as supplies and troops was cooling its heels at Al-Jouf in Saudi Arabia, waiting to make the run north.

It looked like it was going to be waiting a long while. Hawkins had discovered that two immense wadis ran along the ends of the concrete. The dry creekbeds could not be filled without massive amounts of fill and cement; even then, the engineers feared the ground would give way under heavy use. Working with prefab steel mesh, the engineers had managed to lengthen the strip to about fifteen hundred feet. But that was it. They had no chance of getting the strip long enough for the intended operations. Not even Hogs could operate here with a reasonable degree of safety.

"Herky pilot says he could get in if we need him," Hawkins told Doberman and Shotgun after they had shed their survival gear and donned campaign hats against the sun. "But there's no way he can land his C-130 with any sort of load. We're hoping to get a Pave-Low up with fuel for the helicopters tonight; at the moment I have barely enough in case we have to bug out."

"What about us?" asked Doberman.

Hawkins frowned.

"Shit," said Doberman.

"We may be able to run some more fuel up on another Pave-Low tomorrow night," said Hawkins. "Or maybe they can figure out some sort of drop."

"Tomorrow night?"

"Shit, dump some of this coffee in the bladders, Hog'll purr like a kitten," said Shotgun, draining his cup.

"The proximity of Iraqi installations makes Pave-Low flights a precarious proposition," said Wong, belatedly joining the discussion. "The MH-53 family has a significantly large detection profile. They are likely to be seen as well as heard, if not actually scanned by radar. Their flights would compromise the usefulness of the base, especially if more than one craft was required."

"And a Herky Bird wouldn't?" said Doberman.

"A C-130 could, in theory, descend from altitude in a nonapparent trajectory," said Wong.

"Which means what?" Doberman snapped. Intel specialists tended to rub him the wrong way, but Wong was in a class of his own.

"I think he means they could make it look like it was

going somewhere else," said Hawkins. He said it like he not only understood but liked Wong—a truly scary thought.

"Correct. But in any event, I would not like to wager on a C-130 landing here, let alone it taking off," said Wong. "As your landings demonstrated, even the A-10A Thunderbolt II has difficulty, despite its innate short-field capacities."

"Nah," said Shotgun. "We were just trying to make it look tough."

Wong twisted his nose, as if his tongue were a windup toy. "At forward-strip weight, the A-10A needs 396 meters to land and 442 meters to take off. Now, depending on the ordnance configuration and fuel load, wind, ambient temperature—"

"Thanks, Wong, I know the math," snapped Doberman. "I just landed, remember?"

"Face it, Doggie, we're just ground soldiers now," said Shotgun joyfully. "Mud fighters. Snake eaters."

"If you can handle a gun, you can take a turn as a sentry," said Hawkins.

"That's what I'm talking about," said Shotgun. "Give me a 203 and I'll be happy."

Before Doberman could ask what the hell a 203 was, Technical Sergeant Rosen entered the bunker.

"Captains."

Like any experienced sergeant, she said the word in a way that made it seem she was referring to an inferior rank.

"I thought I asked you not to break my planes," she deadpanned.

Doberman felt his face turn red. "Yeah, something jammed up the deceleron. I couldn't get it to deploy at first.

That's why I took the lap. Must've been a lucky shot from somebody on the ground. I didn't feel it."

"Not your plane, sir," said Rosen. "You took some splinters, but it's just a case of bending a little metal back into place. It's Captain O'Rourke's I'm talking about."

"What's wrong with my plane?"

"Aside from the coffee stains on the console," said Rosen, "you have a hole in the hydraulic line."

"No shit," said Shotgun. "I thought the controls felt a little woody."

"Woody? I'm surprised you landed."

"Nah. Come on."

"Well, it's small, so you didn't lose much fluid. But five more minutes and you would have had a hell of a problem. I'm telling you, Captain; you're lucky."

"You're going to fix it, though, right?" asked Shotgun.

"I don't know if I can," said Rosen.

"Shit, we're talking a Hog here," said Shotgun. "All you got to do is stick some bubble gum on the line and fill the reservoir with piss, I'm flyin' in no time."

"There's no bubble gum on this base," Rosen told Shotgun. "I'll be honest with you, I'm not sure I can fix it."

"Fuck."

"If I patch it, we have to worry about having enough fluid."

"There's two separate systems, right?" said Shotgun. "Tie one off, other's good to go."

"Not quite that simple," said Rosen.

"Yeah, but you can do it."

"What I need is something to make a patch," she said. "I need some clamps and a narrow hose, at a minimum."

"Shit, there's probably something you can use on those helos, no?" asked Shotgun.

"No, sir," said Rosen as Hawkins bristled behind her. "And I don't know if Captain Hawkins has told you or not, but there's no Hog juice on this base."

"Use the helo fuel," said Shotgun. "It's jet fuel, right?"

Hawkins glared at him.

"Just an idea," said Shotgun.

"Jet fuel's jet fuel," said Rosen. She looked at Hawkins. "But the helos are low. I don't know if they'd make it down to Saudi if they have to. Their orders are to keep two hours' worth in reserve, and they say they're inside that now."

She glanced at Doberman. Did the glance mean she thought there was more fuel than Hawkins was letting on? Or did it mean something else?

Doberman wanted it to mean something else, something like, *I wish I could kiss you but there are too many Delta types around and they'd get jealous.* Doberman had had the hots for her since Al-Jouf, and he suspected—hoped—the feeling was mutual.

"Why don't you use the fuel you have?" suggested Wong.

"Yeah right," said Doberman. "I landed with maybe ten minutes of reserves."

"Take Captain O'Rourke's fuel as well. Ten minutes plus ten minutes will give you twenty," said Wong. "Enough to make the border. You could meet the tanker, top off, and come back. Once on the ground, half of your fuel could be loaded into Captain O'Rourke's aircraft, allowing him to take off once repairs are completed."

"If repairs *are* completed," said Rosen.

"Ten minutes and ten minutes won't make twenty," said

Doberman. "For one thing, getting off the ground is going to eat up a lot. I doubt there'd even be enough for takeoff."

"You know what, Dog man, I think Braniac's onto something," said Shotgun. "I had a good amount sloshing around when I landed. Must've been three thousand pounds at least. Maybe more. Coulda been five."

"If you had so much fuel, why didn't you fly on to Saudi Arabia?"

"What, and leave you all alone?" Shotgun grinned and shrugged. Five thousand pounds would have been nearly half-full. "We ought to at least check it out. You might be able to do it. Hell, you know every gas gauge ever invented is pessimistic. It's some kind of oil cartel law or somethin'."

"Perhaps a gallon or two might be siphoned from the helicopter reserve," added Wong. "Then replaced when you return."

Hawkins gave a noncommittal grunt.

"Even if we can suck every last drop out and get it into the place, I don't know that you'll have enough to take off and fly to the border, no matter what the gauges say," said Rosen. "I don't know, Captain. You'd be taking a hell of a risk."

She turned her green eyes toward Doberman's. In that instant he knew he could do it. He knew he could do anything—except stay here where he couldn't touch her.

"Yeah, well, let's find out," said Doberman. "I'll be damned if I'm going sit here useless on the ground."

3

Colonel Michael "Skull" Knowlington slid back in his office chair and craned his neck upward so he could stare out the small window of the double-wide trailer that served as Devil Squadron's headquarters. All he could see from this angle was blue sky.

Not very appropriate. But at the moment the colonel lacked the energy to find something else to stare at. He'd just come from the "Bat Cave," where a general in charge of Special Operations had informed him that Lieutenant William James Dixon, temporarily assigned as a ground FAC or forward air controller with a special Delta Force unit, was MIA and presumed killed in Iraq.

Knowlington had been with the Air Force a long time. He'd had three tours in Vietnam in two different aircraft. He'd lost a wingman there, and had punched out once himself. Since then, he'd witnessed three fatal midair mishaps, including one in which he was flying chase. The colonel knew death; he knew how delicately balanced life really was, how the chance movement of a thin wire at the wrong time upended everything. He'd seen death not merely in the lifeless eyes of a pilot tossed from his plane, but in the empty stares of men who'd survived one mission too many, who'd traded their souls to get down to ground safely, only to find the bargain too dear.

And yet, Dixon's death hit him harder than any other. It hit him physically, puncturing his liver like a scalpel plunging into an unanesthetized body. BJ was just a greenhorn kid, a nugget lieutenant not bright enough to steer clear of harebrained Special Ops schemes. He'd volunteered for the Iraq mission—*volunteered, the asshole!*—without Knowlington's permission.

The fact that the kid had sacrificed his own life to save the life of one of the Delta Force team members angered Knowlington even more. It wasn't that he resented the wounded sergeant Dixon had saved; it was the fact that, to Knowlington's way of thinking, neither sacrifice was worth what the mission was supposed to achieve. The Delta teams had been planted to finger Scud missiles for Hogs and other fighter-bombers. In Knowlington's opinion—and in others'—the missiles were tactically useless. The only reason to attack them was political—in his opinion, the exact reason not to proceed.

More than that bothered him, though.

The colonel had banished BJ to a do-nothing desk job in Riyadh the week before as punishment for not giving a full and proper report of a mission on the first day of the air war. At the time it seemed like the wisest thing to do, a harmless slap on the wrist. But it must not have seemed that way to Dixon. The kid must've figured he had to make up for it somehow, even if it meant volunteering to commit suicide.

If Dixon had gone down while flying, Knowlington's insides would not have stung quite so bad. Flying was a difficult business, even under the best circumstances; in combat it was a matter of time and luck versus skill. When you climbed into the cockpit and snugged your hat, you knew you were making a deal with Fortune. You could work to put the odds in your favor, but the fact was that X amount of hours equaled Y amount of problems, and Z percentage of those problems were insoluble, no matter how great a flier you were. Sooner or later, you would have no choice but to go for the yellow handle next to the seat. That was the deal, and at some level, conscious or unconscious, every pilot knew the deal and bought into it.

But dying on the ground, in a firefight he'd never been trained for in a place where he shouldn't have been—what sense did that make? Whose deal was that?

Knowlington felt the bile eating all the way out from his gut to his skin. It seared the rims of his eyes and melted the sensation from his hands.

There was a cure, and he knew it well—three fingers' worth of Jack Daniel's sour mash, straight up in a clear glass tumbler. Three fingers' worth, barely four ounces, just enough to burn the throat going down, just enough fire to sear the acid, snuff it out.

And then?

More and more and more, a never-ending fire. A different kind of deal.

The colonel focused his eyes, straining to see something in the blue rectangle of sky. He had work to do, a lot of work. He had to oversee the squadron's "frag" or fragment of the Air Tasking Order, basically its to-do list for tomorrow's action. He had to make sure he had the planes and the pilots and the ordnance to carry out his portion of the air war. He had to check on his two Hogs at Al-Jouf, assigned to provide air support for the Delta Force at Fort Apache and beyond. He had to find a replacement DO or director of operations, who would serve as the squadron's second in command. There were two or three personnel matters that Sergeant Clyston, his first sergeant, his top crewdog, his capo di capo, wanted to consult on.

He also had to get to the business of notifying Dixon's next of kin.

He wanted to work. But more, he wanted, he needed a drink.

Twenty-two days, nearly to the minute. That was how long it had been.

An immense amount of time.

Skull snapped his eyes away from the blank blue rectangle, forced his hands to move into his desk. He took out the computer sheets with the frag and a lined pad, along with notes and a sortie list.

He'd gone through the frag twice already. He had a plan and a backup plan and a contingency plan. He had the next day's lineup figured out, knew how he was going to rotate the pilots for the next ten days, knew which planes would go where and which would back those up. He had every possible mission configuration covered for the foreseeable future.

Three fingers. Barely a trickle.

An informal AA meeting started at noon every day in one

of the chaplain's quarters in Tent City. If he walked quickly, he could make it.

The Depot, a theoretically off-limits black-market club in a bomb shelter just outside the base, lay in the opposite direction, exactly 713 long strides away.

Skull put the paperwork away, took a long breath, and rose from his desk, not quite sure which direction he would take.

4

Sometime in the early 1960s, above the steaming jungles of Vietnam, a young man pushed the controls of an ancient A-1 Skyraider and fell through a wall of small-arms fire to drop a stick of bombs on a squad of Viet Cong rebels. The bombs fell with uncanny precision, killing enough enemy soldiers to allow a small patrol of Vietnamese regulars and their American advisor to escape the ambush that had trapped them.

In the grand scheme of a horrific war, it was an insignificant event—a few more people dead on either side, one way or the other, didn't make much difference in Vietnam. But this bombing run was very different than most others up to that point—it was at close range, damn accurate, and it did what it was supposed to do: kill bad guys. With all due respect to the brave men who'd flown missions in fast-moving jets in the months before the Spad's sortie, these were radical developments.

And they were radical not because this particular pilot was very well trained or especially brave, though it goes without saying that he was both. What was radical was his plane—a geezer engineered during World War II and pulled through the air by technology the Wright brothers would have been familiar with.

Intended as a torpedo bomber, the Skyraider could carry a lot of bombs and provided a very stable platform to drop them from. It was also completely outclassed by jets in every performance category, a slow-moving, low-flying aerial barge.

Which proved to be a serious asset. Flying lower and slower than a jet meant it was better at blowing little stuff up. Little stuff like tanks and machine-gun nests and armored cars and mortar sites—exactly the sort of stuff that mattered the most in that war. And, in fact, in any war.

There were more Spad missions after that first one, a lot more. And it didn't take the brass long to realize that if the Air Force was going to be in the business of supporting grunts—not that they unanimously agreed it should, but never mind—it needed planes that were more like the A-1, less like the high-tech, go-fast, never-see-ya F-4s, *et al.* The Spad's success led, more or less directly, to the Attack Experimental Program of 1967, a program that eventually resulted in the A-10A.

Among the many specifications for the AX was the ability to take off from "austere" forward air bases. Fort Apache was about as austere and forward as air bases got. And while the plank of concrete Doberman was about to walk was at least five hundred feet longer than the original

AX specifications called for, the Hog was quite a bit heavier as well.

Uglier, too. But ugly was good.

Snug inside the titanium hull of the ground pounder, Doberman leaned toward the side of the Hog and gave his ground crew—Rosen—a thumbs-up. The plane had been positioned at the very edge of the runway, fanny over the sand, nose into the wind. Hawkins had anted up a few gallons and Shotgun's tanks had held more fuel than they'd hoped; still, with a good clean takeoff Doberman would have under a half hour to make the rendezvous with the tanker. The AWACS airborne command post coordinating the air war had been alerted, and he'd been promised priority at the tanker—but Doberman knew from experience that could be a difficult if not impossible promise to keep.

Trained as an engineer, Doberman tended to break things down by numbers. The numbers in this case said no way. But he'd been through so much in the last few days that he was almost comfortable ignoring them.

He took a breath, and told himself he was going for it. He needed a clean crank from the plane's starter; he needed to take off the second his wicks lit.

Another breath. Then his fingers flew around the cockpit, push-buttoning himself into gear. The turbines sputtered a half moment, then caught; he was off the brake, asking the Hog for full kick-butt-and-let's-go power as the whine of the GE powerplants revved up and down his spine.

The Hog gave it to him, winding her engines with a cheerful roar. No A-10A liked sitting on the ground, and this one seemed to relish the challenge ahead—she leaped into the fresh breeze more than three hundred feet before the specs said she ought to, snorting at the fools who'd underestimated her.

Doberman's hand nudged the throttle back gently as he brought the wheels up, adjusting, adjusting, adjusting, determined to give the plane just enough fuel to fly. The Hog seemed to understand, holding steady as her pilot banked toward the south. She jostled in the air until she found a wind current to help push her along.

Earlier in the air war, heavy weather had clogged the sky; the winter had been unusually stormy, even considering that they were in the middle of what passed for the rainy season. Today there was nothing but blue, punctuated above Doberman's canopy by the contrails of allied jets crisscrossing as they sought to eradicate Saddam's ability to fight. Over 2,700 sorties would be made today, bringing the war to Iraq with unprecedented ferocity.

The radio was heavy with traffic, wingmen offering each other advice and reassurance, flights warning others what lay ahead, controllers scrambling fighters to meet different threats. Doberman caught some chatter from a group of F-111s well behind and above him on his squadron frequency; the bombers were making their way back from an open house hosted by Saddam's interior ministry. This was apparently the first time they'd attacked during the day, and the pilots were making jokes about how they had to close their eyes so they knew what to do.

Doberman nudged the stick, pushing his nose to the proper compass point slotted in the thick dial in front of his chest. He nailed it, then took a quick run through the fuel and navigational data and glanced at his kneepad, where he'd made a cheat sheet of his fuel calculations to show him whether he was going to make it or not. He was right on course with fifteen minutes to go to the tanker and four minutes of fuel beyond that, assuming Rosen's measurements and not the somewhat pessimistic gauge were correct.

Had to go with the girl.

He hit his first way marker and made a minor correction. It was just a straight run south now. The course would take him over two known Iraqi positions, and possibly others as well. Doberman checked his altitude; he was at twelve thousand feet.

"Devil One this is Tiger," said the AWACS controller, checking in.

Doberman acknowledged. The controller confirmed that the tanker, an Air Force KC-135 known as "Bluebeard," had been alerted and would be ready at the northern end of its track. The planes circled in patterns similar to extended oval racetracks. Depending on the track and circumstances, several tankers could be lined up, with half a dozen thirsty planes queuing to "tank." Doberman was getting seriously special treatment due to his mission and his fuel state. The KC-135—basically a 707 with jet fuel instead of passengers—not only had to fly to the northernmost point of her orbit just in time to meet him, she was coming down from her usual twenty or twenty-five thousand feet as well. And nobody was going to give the crew a medal for the extra danger.

Doberman thanked the AWACS controller and worked his eyes carefully through his instruments, triple-checking the gauges and indicators that accessorized his office. With eight minutes left to the border, he was just about to dial into the tanker's radio frequency when a warning from the AWACS boomed in his ears.

"Devil One, snap ninety," the controller shouted tersely.

It was an impossible command, directing him to take a sharp turn he couldn't afford to make. Immediately, the radar warning receiver on his dash showed him the reason—a ground radar had begun tracking him, undoubtedly with the intention of firing missiles in his direction.

The controller's next transmission was overrun by a Wild Weasel, a specially modified F-4 Phantom tasked with taking out SAMs. The words flew by so fast Doberman could only get the gist, but that was enough—an SA-2 battery they'd thought dead had just snapped back to life.

Worse, it was launching.

Correct that: had launched. Two visual sightings, confirmed by radar, confirmed by Doberman's own eyes as he glanced involuntarily to the left. Two small white-and-black puffballs erupted three miles ahead of his left wing. Two dark black slivers arced out of the smoke, and Doberman didn't have to glance at a cheat sheet or run the numbers in his head to know it was already too late to run away, even if his tanks had been overflowing with fuel.

5

With his plane temporarily grounded and no Dunkin'
Donuts franchise in sight, Shotgun figured he'd kill a few
hours by taking Hawkins up on the sentry thing. Which he
assumed was a serious offer, even though the captain had
been smirking when he made it. So he went and asked him
about it after Doberman took off.

"Uh, with all due respect, Captain," said Hawkins. "And
absolutely no offense intended, but you're Air Force."

"Yeah, that's what I'm talking about," said Shotgun. "Do
I get one of those 203 grenade launchers? Or do I have to
settle for an MP-5?"

"Neither."

"Have to use what I came with, huh?" Shotgun slapped
the holster of his customized .45, which was wedged inside
his customized flightsuit. "Fair enough."

"Are you out of your fucking mind?"

"Why?" asked Shotgun. "Is that a job requirement?"

A Delta Force sergeant listening nearby took Hawkins aside. Shotgun waited as they stepped a few paces away, talking in voices too soft for him to hear. Finally, Hawkins turned back to the pilot and pointed at him.

"Don't get yourself hurt," Hawkins yelled. Shaking his head, he went off toward the helos at the other end of the base.

"Captain, my name is Sergeant Coors," the NCO informed Shotgun. His mouth spread into the standard-issue Spec Ops smile: half sneer, half inside joke. "I'll be your tour guide this afternoon, if you're up to it."

"Shit yeah, I'm up to it," said Shotgun. He pounded the sergeant's shoulder to emphasize his point. Coors was about Shotgun's height but not nearly his weight; the Delta operator grimaced and nodded.

"We have a post out this way we need manned," said the sergeant, leading the way.

"Great, Beerman," said Shotgun, following. "You sergeants are all right."

"Well, thank you, sir. Some of my best friends are captains."

"What'd you say to Hawkins to convince him?"

"I told him I was going to run your ass ragged," said Coors. "Sir."

"Shit, my ass is so big it's going to take a lot more than you," said Shotgun. "But you take your best shot."

Coors led Shotgun across the cement landing strip to what seemed to be a pair of low sand dunes. In fact, the dunes had been constructed by the sappers from canvas and dirt to conceal Fort Apache's small motor pool, which consisted of one slightly banged-up FAV.

Officially, the acronym stood for "fast attack vehicle." Unofficially, it stood for a lot of other things, all of which began with an "f" word other than "fast."

The craft was a two-tiered dune buggy straight out of *The Road Warrior*. With a low profile and extra-large mufflers, the FAV was a Go Kart with guns. The driver manned the bottom cage; the passenger sat on a platform behind him, working a machine gun, TOW missile setup, and maybe a grenade launcher.

Unfortunately, this particular unit had been stripped of weapons. It did, however, move pretty fast. Grit sandpapered Shotgun's face as the FAV revved northeastward to a high point along the western wadi that marked one side of the base. Though technically still part of the desert, the wasteland around Apache was far more solid than farther south in Saudi Arabia. There were short scrubby bushes and occasional outcroppings of something similar to weedy grass.

There were also a lot of rocks. Coors didn't miss one, jostling Shotgun's head against the tubular steel backrest. They stopped next to what seemed to be a large pile of shifting sand, but proved to be a yellow-brown tarp on a row of sandbags when Shotgun jumped on it from the top of the FAV. He'd never have thought sandbags could be so hard.

"This is a fallback position," Coors explained, gesturing with the MP-5 he had slung over his shoulder with a long strap. The bags made a slight arc that would provide cover for one or two men. He thumbed north. "Where we're going is closer to the road."

A gray-black line edged in front of a series of low hills about three miles away. Shotgun realized it was a highway.

"We leave the FAV here so it can't be seen. Remember where this cache is—there's a radio and weapons if you need them." He pointed in the distance. "It's the high point near the dried-out stream."

"You got a little ol' M-16 in there I can borrow?"

"Sorry, sir, but the idea here is not to do anything that's going to attract attention, if you know what I mean. The idea is just to watch what's going on, not to start firing willy-nilly. No offense."

Coors obviously meant to offend him, but Shotgun let it pass. He'd dealt with this sort of prejudice before. People assumed that because you were a Hog pilot, you liked to blow things up, and because you liked to blow things up, you wouldn't exercise proper judgment when a fat target presented itself. You'd just go blasting away and worry about the consequences later.

Which was true enough, now that he thought about it. The sergeant took a large rucksack from the FAV and began trudging along the top of the wadi in the direction of the road. About three hundred yards from the FAV, Coors stopped in front of a group of small boulders.

Shotgun stooped down, trying to find an opening in the dirt. He had to hand it to the commandos—this hide was even better than the last one. It was completely invisible, even up close.

"I give up," he said, straightening. "Where is it?"

"Where's what?"

"The hide."

"Right here," said Coors with a grin. He dropped the rucksack and pulled a small folding shovel from the side.

"Have fun," he said, handing it to Shotgun. "I'll be back in a half hour."

"Hold on, Beerman," said Shotgun. He grabbed the trooper by the arm and spun him back as he started away. "What's with the truck?"

"Truck?"

"A hundred yards past that bend," Shotgun said, pointing. "Down the dip in the road. See the edge of the roof?"

Coors couldn't see the roof, but his whole manner changed instantly. He dropped to his knees, removing his Steiner field glasses from the rucksack. Shotgun squatted next to him, waiting while the sergeant adjusted the glasses and scanned back and forth. Finally, the pilot leaned over and helped aim the glasses into the right spot.

"Fuck, how did you see that?" asked Coors finally. "That's three miles away."

"Two-point-seven," said Shotgun. "If we go up a little further, we can get a better view."

Without answering, the sergeant began to trot to his right, his head ducked slightly to keep his profile relatively low. He stopped about fifty yards away, with a much better angle.

"Tanker truck," said the trooper. "Shit. Not moving."

"Yeah. You mind if I take a look?" asked Shotgun.

The sergeant hesitated for a second, then handed him the glasses. Shotgun stood slowly. The sun was behind him, which silhouetted him but prevented any chance reflection off the glasses. It seemed like a fair trade.

"Doesn't seem to be anybody in the cab," said Shotgun. "You got the hill right behind him. Maybe he's taking a leak."

"Long leak," grumbled Coors.

"You can flank him from that hill."

Coors tugged his pants leg. "Sit down and let me think about this a minute."

While the sergeant was thinking, Shotgun unholstered his pistol. The Colt 1911 Government Model had come from a factory maybe thirty or forty years before, but its gizzards had been completely replaced with custom components. It also had a beavertail grip safety courtesy of a South Carolina gunsmith Shotgun had met while waiting at a Mickey D's a few years back. Ordinarily, Shotgun did his own work, but you could always trust someone who supersized his fries.

"Okay," said the sergeant, picking up his submachine gun. "I'm going to double back a hundred yards or so, then cross the road. I'll come up that rise behind him where I can get a better view."

"And what am I doing?"

"You're going for help if I get in trouble."

Shotgun figured there was no sense arguing with the sergeant, especially since Coors had already begun trotting away. He folded his arms in front of his chest, watching as the sergeant cut back across the terrain and then angled for the road. Even though he was half crouching, wearing a rucksack and carrying a submachine gun, Coors made good time, disappearing from Shotgun's line of sight in a little more than ten minutes.

The pilot waited a full thirty seconds after that, then began his own scoot toward the fuel truck, aiming to get close enough to help in case there was any trouble. Between the wadi and the slope, he had cover for a bit over a mile and a half, which meant he was still a good quarter mile away when somebody started shouting and firing an automatic rifle from the rocks at the edge of the hill.

6

He found himself at the Depot, sitting at the long, black Formica bartop, staring at a pyramid of whiskey bottles. All of his old friends were there, as if gathered for a reunion— Seagram's and Windsor Canadian, Mount Royal, Rebel Yell, Heaven Hill, Merritt, Jim Beam, Old Crow, Maker's Mark, Ten High, Jameson, Booker's, Grand-Dad, and Wild Turkey.

And Jack, luscious Jack Daniel's in all his glory, green and black, a serious, serious friend.

There was a large double shot glass in front of him. Filled to the white line near the rim.

Was it his first? His third? His fifth? Was he drunk already?

Skull eased forward on the bar stool. What difference did

it make if this was his first or his twenty-first—he was already drunk on the fumes.

Change from a twenty on the bar next to him. A ten and a five and three ones.

Two bucks for a double shot?

Jesus, no wonder guys said this place had sprung whole from somebody's wet dream.

Colonel Knowlington bent toward the drink, thinking about Dixon and the day he'd sent him to Riyadh.

Shit. He could still see the kid's face, white as a nun's bedsheet, admitting he'd screwed up.

The kid had come clean. That was who he was—naive, foolish, but honest. A damn good kid, brimming with potential, the kind of kid the Air Force needed. The kind of kid Skull had been once, if only for a very short time.

It sucked shit to lose him.

Knowlington fingered the glass. It sucked shit to lose every goddamn man he'd lost, every wingman, every friend, every acquaintance, everybody he'd had to order into battle. It sucked shit for anybody to die in war—even the goddamn bastards on the other side, the poor slobs working for a madman, just doing their job.

His throat contracted, waiting for the bourbon.

Twenty-two days since he'd last felt the pleasant burn. Twenty-two sober days.

Why? So he could send more good kids to their deaths?

No. So he could keep his head clear. So people who needed him could look at him and nod. So they could trust him, not have to worry about his decisions.

Fuck that naive bullshit.

Skull brought the glass to his mouth. There was a sweet sting on his lips.

No. Not for this. Not for this.

Slowly, carefully, he set the drink back on the bar and walked out quietly, leaving his money and the full glass, his first glass in twenty-two days, behind.

7

Doberman closed his hand around the control stick and narrowed his focus, staring through the heads-up display at the empty blue sky before him. His threat indicator showed clearly that the enemy missiles were gunning for him. His electronic countermeasures—supplied by an AN/ALQ-119 ECM pod carried on the Hog's right wing—were busting their transistors in an attempt to confuse the missiles' Fong Song F radar and guidance system. Ordinarily, Doberman would jink and jive to increase the odds of escaping, but if he did that, he'd run out of gas about thirty seconds after the missiles passed.

He bent his head forward and back, breathing slowly and willing the jammer to do its thing.

Meanwhile, a Wild Weasel swept in to kill the installation that had launched the missiles. A backseat whizzo in an ancient Phantom leaned against the cockpit's iron wall as his powerful radar got a lock on the enemy trailers; he punched the trigger and kicked off an AGM-88 High-Speed Anti-Radiation (HARM) missile toward the Iraqi installation.

One of the SA-2s fell away. But the other kept coming. He saw it, a dark toothpick growing in the bottom left corner of his canopy mirror. It was close now, smelling him. Doberman felt the muscles in his shoulder tighten, snapping so taut he felt his throat close. He could see the damn thing coming for him, getting bigger and bigger.

"All right," he said to himself. "Better to run out of gas than get whacked by a telephone pole."

He leaned hard on the stick and juiced the throttle, whacking out electronic chaff at the same time. The metallic tinsel unfolded in the air, a shadow to help confuse whatever was still guiding the missile, make it think the Hog was still straight and level.

Maybe that worked. Maybe the HARM missile that took out the ground radar guidance system managed to disrupt the SA-2 before it went terminal. Maybe one of the electronic warfare planes flying farther south hit just the right chord of confusion at just the right moment. Or maybe Doberman's incredible luck continued to hold.

Whatever.

The Hog slid down toward the earth, eating g's as she stomped toward the yellow sand. The SA-2 climbed past it, passing through the tinsel and then flying for nearly a thousand more feet before her nose started to wobble. The wobble turned into a shudder, and the warhead exploded.

Two hundred and eighty-seven pounds of high explosive makes a fair amount of boom, but Doberman was well out of range by the time the missile detonated. When he realized he'd escaped, he pulled the plane back, swooping back for his course while he checked his fuel and position on the INS. Then he checked the numbers against his chart.

If his math was right, he had less than thirty seconds to the border and another five miles to the tanker.

And sixty-two seconds of fuel beyond that.

Doberman started to laugh uncontrollably.

"I'm going to make it," he said, as if it were a joke. He tapped his finger on his pad. "I'm going to make it. I can't believe it."

He laughed and he laughed, and the only thing that stopped him was a radio call from Bluebeard, the tanker, which was on an intercept dead ahead.

"Devil One, I see you but I'm going to need you to come up to flight level twelve," said the tanker pilot. "That's twelve angels, twelve thousand feet."

"Nah, we'll meet halfway," said Doberman.

If the tanker pilot thought he was out of his mind—which he had every right to—he didn't say. Instead, he threw out his landing gear to help him slow down and put the big Boeing into a steep bank, diving and turning at the same time. No aerobatics pilot ever performed so tricky a maneuver—or one half so beautiful to the audience.

"I appreciate that," said Doberman, kissing his throttle to inch up his speed and catch the tanker. He tried to relax his shoulders, relax everything but his eyes, which were hard bullets homing in on the director lights beneath the tanker that told him whether he was going to make the connection or not. He had an extreme angle but there wasn't time for a second try. He pushed the Hog a bit too far to the left, came back heavy with his rudder, eyes narrowed to pinpoints.

The Hog's nose nailed the nozzle with a satisfying thud. Fuel flowed nearly instantaneously.

Doberman glanced at his watch and then at his pad.

According to the cheat sheet, he'd run out of fuel thirty-two seconds ago.

8

For a desert, the ground was damn hard. Stinkin' Iraqis couldn't even get sand right, for crying out loud.

Shotgun cursed for the millionth time, pushing himself forward on his elbows and knees, eyes pinned on the Iraqi holed up in the rocks a few yards from the tanker truck. The man seemed to have an endless supply of bullets and didn't mind spraying them around, though fortunately he was firing toward the hill, not Shotgun. The Iraqi was so interested in Coors—or whatever he was shooting at—that he hadn't bothered to even glance in Shotgun's direction.

The pilot was no more than a hundred yards from the Iraqi, but no matter what you did to a .45 it was still a .45; a hundred yards with a pistol on a target range was a guess-your-weight shot, and this was hardly a target range. Shotgun waited for the Iraqi to begin firing again; as soon as he did, Shotgun threw himself forward, collapsing as the final round stopped echoing against the low hills. That brought him nearly ten yards closer.

At this rate, Saddam would be on work release from a federal pen before Shotgun got close enough to nail the bastard.

The funny thing was, Coors hadn't fired, at least not that Shotgun had heard. That could mean that the Iraqi was just dinking shadows in the hills while the Delta operator flanked him.

It could also mean he was lying on the slope bleeding to death.

Shotgun waited for the Iraqi to fire again. The burst was shorter this time; the pilot managed only five yards before his belly flop.

This much up and down was going to wear his flightsuit out. Then he'd be forced into Spec Ops jammies. Okay up here maybe, but what would they say back in Devil Squadron's readyroom? They'd haul him right over to the Depot and make him buy everybody in the squadron a round of drinks.

While he waited for the Iraqi to fire again, Shotgun decided the liability to his ego, let alone his wallet, didn't permit any more fooling around. As soon as the Iraqi began shooting, he got up and began walking double time, not bothering to stop or even crouch as the last round of Russian-made ammo echoed against the shallow hills.

He got maybe forty yards before he heard the muffled, not-quite-delicate sound of Coors's MP-5. The Iraqi immediately rose from the rocks and returned fire.

Clear shot. Too far at fifty yards, but hey.

Shotgun squeezed off a round, cursing as the Iraqi jerked

around. The man dropped his gun and fell, struck in the shoulder.

"I knew I was going to miss," the pilot grumbled. •

Winged, the Iraqi scrambled for his gun. Shotgun waited until the soldier squared the rifle toward him before firing again. This time he nàiled him in the middle of the forehead.

"I thought I told you to stay back," Coors screamed as he scrambled down the rocks.

"Yeah, you're welcome."

"Fuck you," said the sergeant.

"Not today," said Shotgun. He scanned the area quickly, making sure there were no other Iraqis. The dead man's position was in the shadow of the truck and hills, which had probably made him hard for Coors to see as he came down.

"Yeah, well, thanks," muttered the trooper as Shotgun slipped his gun back into his holster. "I didn't see him when I checked out the area from the ridge and then I got sloppy. Raghead musta heard a rock or dirt I kicked. He couldn't get me but he had me pinned down. I owe ya one."

"I'll collect," said Shotgun. He snatched up the soldier's AK-47 and started back toward the truck. "Lucky there wasn't any traffic, huh?"

Coors shrugged. "They mostly drive at night."

"Yeah." Shotgun laughed. "What do you figure the odds that he's carrying jet fuel?"

"Prohibitive," said Coors.

Shotgun disagreed. Leaving a tanker full of Hog juice at their door would be just the sort of neighborly gesture Saddam might use to entice Devil Squadron to go home.

It wouldn't work, of course, but it was nice to be appreciated.

"I think it's water," said Coors after clambering up the tanker to peer through the manhole at the top. "It ain't gas or oil. No wait."

He stuck his head down into the interior of the dull steel tank. The skin was marked by dents and dings; if it had ever been polished, the finish had long since worn away. The top was mated to a ZIL 130 chassis. What seemed to be military markings had been painted over with inelegant swaths of gray paint, completing the early-junkyard look.

"Water?" Shotgun asked.

Coors pulled his head out with a laugh. "I think it's milk. Still fresh, too. Or at least it don't stink."

"Now all we need's a truck full of cookies," said Shotgun, hauling himself up the ladder to have a look.

He leaned into the manhole and took a whiff. It smelled like milk, though on the watery side and with a metallic hint.

"Milk," he declared. "But you aren't going to want to drink it. Be okay for dunking. Yeah." He straightened, considering the scent. Milk wasn't his beverage of choice. "Wouldn't ruin good coffee with it. No. Dunking would be okay. But not just any dunking—have to be hard cookies, like Italian biscotti or Russian rusks. Donuts are out," he added as he jumped down to look over the rest of the truck. "Because they're going to soak in too much moisture and that's going to bring the aftertaste with it. What you need is something with granules and surface area. So we're talking biscotti. Hard cookies. Evaporation and crumbs, that's what I'm talking about."

Coors pretended not to be interested. "What do you think they were doing way out here with milk?"

Shotgun shrugged, looking into the cab to make sure it

wasn't booby-trapped before opening it. "Maybe they couldn't get beer."

Outside of a screwdriver and a map, the cab was empty. There didn't seem to be anything wrong with the truck that a half hour in a car wash wouldn't fix. Still, ZILs weren't known for their reliability and it wasn't until he had monkeyed with the carburetor for a few minutes that Shotgun realized the driver had simply run out of gas.

"You think we can siphon some out of the FAV?" he asked the sergeant. The old Soviet-era transports used petrol rather than diesel.

"Won't have to. Got a spare gas tank lashed on the top. You wait here and I'll be back."

"Wait a second," said Shotgun. "You owe me one, remember?"

"Yeah?"

"So I'm collecting."

"You're collecting by walking back to the FAV?"

"And driving it here. I'll be back before you have the body buried in the rocks over there."

Coors laughed. "You're a piece of work, Captain."

"Nah. Just a Hog driver," answered Shotgun, returning his one-fingered salute.

9

Dixon's mouth, throat, and stomach had seared together, parched and burned by hunger and thirst and heat. The only part of him that felt good was his fingers. They were curled around the stock of the Kalashnikov.

If there had been other Iraqis near the quarry or bunker, they hadn't followed him. Alone and seemingly unnoticed, he trudged eastward, paralleling the highway by about a hundred yards. At first he crouched low to the ground, huddling as close to the scrubby vegetation as possible. Soon, however, he realized there was no one nearby to see him, and the open ground would give him plenty of warning if a vehicle approached. He gradually came out of his crouch, walking slightly stooped over and then finally upright, continuing to turn back and forth, checking his six like the trained fighter pilot he was.

Dixon kicked at the dirt. It seemed thicker stuff than the sandy grit and fine dust back near the quarry. It was the kind of stuff that might almost be farmable—or at least hold enough promise to ruin a man once the summer came. There were irrigation ditches on the other side of the road; a few of them had water at the bottom, though most were dry. In the distance Dixon could see a small hovel which he took to be a farmhouse. Beyond that on his side of the highway was a low set of hills, about five miles off. The hills were gray rather than brown or red. He assumed that meant there were bushes or trees on them; that would mean enough under-ground water for a town or settlement of some sort. Dixon debated whether to walk to it or not. He was hungry and he had to find food, but if there was food there would be Iraqis.

He had to eat, and soon. And he didn't figure he could live off the land. His few days in survival training seemed more like a visit to an amusement park than anything useful to him now.

Dixon was approaching the Cornfield, a predesignated spot his Delta team had used to land a pair of helicopters the night before. They'd been ambushed there; he'd watched the firefight from the hill near the NBC bunker, then come to rescue one of the survivors.

Last night, it had taken less than an hour to get this far. Now it seemed as if it had taken all day.

He glanced at his watch before remembering it had stopped earlier.

The sun wasn't quite halfway down in the sky. Two o'clock? Three?

Dixon could see the top of a wrecked APC south of the road. Other hulks lay beyond it. He decided to go there; he might find food or more weapons or even something he could use to contact one of the other Delta teams operating in Iraq. He turned and began walking directly south toward the highway. Suddenly he broke into a trot and then began running full force. The belt of AK-47 clips jostled against his chest and stomach. One fell off; he left it and kept going, off balance and out of control, running for nearly a quarter of a mile until he slid down the sharp embankment of a dry creekbed. He threw himself against the other side, pulling himself up with his rifle and free hand, stumbling again and then starting to walk toward the APC about thirty yards away.

The drive mechanism had been twisted out from the chassis, opening like a bizarre metal tulip that protruded from the once-smooth side of the truck. The sight of the jagged metal sobered him; when he was five yards away he dropped to his knees, finally catching his breath and regaining his sense.

His eyes like microscopes, he began scanning the Cornfield for an enemy. Finally, he approached the APC, his finger tensing against the trigger of the assault rifle. He moved the barrel back and forth, as if expecting another flower to burst from the metal and reveal a gunner taking aim at him.

A ruined tank sat beyond the APC, maybe thirty yards farther from the road on his right. He began sidestepping toward it, moving the rifle back and forth as if he'd been taking fire from both sides. Then he turned and ran as fast as he could toward the tank, his last dregs of adrenaline flooding into his legs and head. AK-47 ready, he sidestepped around the blackened frame, approaching the front of the turret as if its long-barreled gun had not been shattered in two.

When he was positive there was no one hiding behind or inside the tank, Dixon stepped up onto the back of the vehicle to inspect it. A small bomb or missile had landed near the center of the chassis, ripping a mushroom of metal from the tank's innards. Dixon leaned in carefully, worried that he might cut himself on the shards. Plastic soot covered the interior, a gritty mud that had coagulated and cooled after the initial explosion and fire. A hand, its fingers extended but its thumb missing, lay on its wrist against a thick lump of metal at the front. The rest of the body was gone.

Dixon stepped back, sliding down to one knee behind the turret as he surveyed the battlefield from the Iraqis' vantage point. Greatly outnumbered, the American fire team had briefly held a small hill fifty feet high to his right, but had fought most of the battle in and around a series of ditches directly in front of the tank. Only the arrival of the helicopters and Devil Squadron Hogs had saved the day.

Dixon jumped off the tank and made his way to the hill; it would give him a good view of the rest of the area. As he climbed it he realized he hadn't seen any dead bodies yet.

There were no bodies here either, nor could he see any from the top. The only sign of the battle on the hill was a crater on the southeastern corner of the summit. The dirt in the center was tinged red, as if the earth had bled.

As he stood at the edge of the crater, Dixon's feet began to slip. He managed to throw his weight backward just enough so that he fell down as if plopping into a seat.

He stayed in the hole for a minute, eyes staring into the sky. Faint contrails teased him; twenty or thirty thousand feet above, allied planes were carrying on the war, oblivious to his existence or plight.

Hunger pushed Dixon back to his feet. The lieutenant resumed his search, methodically going to the rest of the burned-out vehicles. The fact that no bodies remained meant the Iraqis must have come through already; it was unlikely he would find anything useful. Still, he kept looking. A Ural 6x6 sat almost unscathed nearly a quarter of a mile from the rest of the vehicles. He found a small metal canteen near it. He juggled it in his hand and, though he didn't hear anything, unscrewed it and held it upside down over his mouth anyway.

A trickle of water surprised his tongue. The liquid felt like hot pebbles, burning holes in his mouth, and then it was gone. He gulped air, and his thirst became a fire, ravaging his body. Canteen in one hand and rifle in the other, Dixon ran to a stream bed a hundred yards south of the battlefield. But he found only dust.

He'd been here before, on this spot, last night. He'd kicked ice. Where was it?

He walked along the dead stream bed. The day had warmed to near fifty, perhaps more. Ice would have melted, but there must be water. It couldn't have evaporated; he couldn't have imagined it.

Dixon must have spent nearly a half hour searching without finding anything. Finally, he whipped the metal bottle down against the rocks. He kicked at the ground and took the rifle and rammed it against the dirt, screaming and cursing.

A voice at the back of his head told him it was a foolish thing to do.

His father's voice, rising from his sickbed. A voice he hadn't heard in many months. A voice that hadn't been coherent in a much longer time, one that could never offer advice. His father had been in a mental institution since Dixon was ten or eleven.

But the voice was right. And whether it was a temporary hallucination or a memory or Dixon's own conscience disguising itself, it helped him catch hold of himself. He sat down, pulling his shirt out from his pants to rub the barrel of the gun clean. Then he got up and retrieved the canteen. Examining it, he found a fresh dent but no real damage; he stuffed it in his pocket.

As he did he saw a small brown box on the side of the wadi, next to a twisted brown bush. Dixon approached it warily; carefully, he scanned the area, made sure he was alone, then knelt and looked it over for booby traps. When he didn't see any, he reached to his belt and unsheathed his combat knife. He punched it into the earth near the box, then began moving it around the ground, hoping that if there *was* a booby trap he'd somehow manage to find it before setting it off. When he didn't find anything, he stood back, and used the AK-47 to poke the box. Nothing happened, and he finally picked it up.

It was an ammo box, and inside were several banana clips of 7.62mm ammo for the assault gun.

He would have much preferred water or food.

Dixon tucked the box under his arm and began walking slowly along the wadi. The stream bed intersected an irrigation ditch a few yards ahead; he turned and walked down the ditch, realizing it was deeper than the wadi. A hundred yards down, past two or three other ditches in the network, he finally saw a pool of water.

Fear welled up from his stomach with every step, clamping itself down like a force trying to keep him from moving. He slid to his knees and unscrewed the top of the canteen, lowering it to the surface of the water. There was at least six inches; he filled the canteen only halfway before rising. He intended on pouring the water over his fingers, to see if it was clean, but as he tilted the metal bottle his thirst jerked his hand up and he poured it nearly straight down into his mouth, every part of him trembling. He did it two more times, silt and grit rubbing against his teeth, choking in his throat.

Nothing liquid had ever tasted as good. He leaned back, balancing on his haunches; finally, he put the rifle down next to the ammo box and removed the campaign hat from his head, soaking it and then wringing it over his face.

As he straightened he heard trucks on the road a half mile away. He pulled the hat down, took the gun and the ammo box, and crawled up to watch them pass.

Except they didn't pass. They slowed and then stopped along the highway. He raised his head as high as he dared and saw someone running toward the Ural truck he had inspected before. The man shouted something and two or three others got out of a white pickup and came over.

Dixon couldn't see what they were doing. The pickup truck was part of a convoy of four or five vehicles, one of which was an APC.

At the tail end were two tractor-trailers with long tarps covering their loads.

He'd stared at them for nearly five minutes before he realized he was looking at a pair of Scud missiles.

By then, the Iraqis had concluded they couldn't do anything with the 6x6 and had returned to their vehicles. Dixon rose; he watched the pickup jerk ahead, then the APC. Black smoke puffed from the exhausts of the lead Scud carrier as the motor revved.

Belatedly, he pulled the assault rifle to his shoulder and aimed at the truck. He had it in his sights, but he was so far away that even if he managed to hit it, the bullet would barely graze the canvas.

Better to follow, get close, find a way to destroy it.

Madness.

But what else was there left for him to do? Stay here and die of starvation?

Die for a purpose, at least. Better to go out in a blaze of glory than starve. Or worse, be found alive but passed out. The Iraqis would use him. That would be worse than torture, worse than death.

Dixon shouldered his rifle and walked back up the low hill to study the area ahead. He couldn't be sure, but it appeared that the Iraqi vehicles were following a turn in the road just beyond the hills in the distance.

There'd be food if there was a village or settlement there. His stomach would stop hurting.

He'd have to kill for it. Kill to eat, to survive.

Dixon shrugged, as if he'd been debating with himself. Killing to survive meant he might kill civilians.

So be it. There were no more civilians as far as he was concerned. Civilians were his father and mother, back home in the States.

His father. Mom was gone.

Could he kill his dad, standing face-to-face, shoot him if his own life depended on it? If he didn't know him?

If he couldn't, if he wouldn't, how could he shoot anyone?

He thought of the Iraqi he'd put out of his misery earlier. Was it mercy or murder?

Dixon opened the ammo box and stuffed the extra clips into the belt and his pants. Pushing himself forward, he stumbled once or twice but kept moving, gaining momentum as he went.

10

When Kevin Hawkins was seven years old, his Irish grand-mother came to stay with him. Within her first hour at the house, she had introduced him to stud poker and Earl Grey tea. Hawkins gave up poker when he joined the Army, but the Delta Force captain's appreciation of the perfumed tea had only grown since basic training. Sipping a cup as he crouched at the edge of Fort Apache's makeshift runway, he felt his fatigue drifting into the nearby sand. The bergamot-scented black liquid worked like an amphetamine, pumping him up, restoring him, at least temporarily, more com-pletely than eight hours of sleep.

Hawkins watched as a dark green vulture approached from the south. Fifty feet off the ground, the vulture began a wide turn to the east, then swung back toward the runway where Hawkins sipped his tea. The wind began to pick up;

the vulture stuttered over the desert. It was an ugly bird, ungainly and fidgety, all wing and head. And then it wasn't a bird at all, it was an A-10A Warthog landing with a fresh load of fuel. The long, straight wings grew as the plane's segmented ailerons and flaps deployed; the nosewheel folded out like a clock pendulum stopping mid-swing.

The plane landed so close Hawkins could feel the heat from the brakes as it screeched past on the mesh his engineers had laid to cover holes in the concrete strip. The Hog's dark hull weaved slightly as the plane halted at the edge of the ravine. It was a reminder that he'd failed.

As good as Hawkins's team was, the immense wadis at either end of the concrete strip limited the makeshift strip to exactly 1,607 feet. That made it too short for the C-130 supply and gunships they'd hoped to base here in support of Scud hunters. Without them, there was no sense staying. It was too great a risk for too little reward. More than a dozen American and British Scud hunting teams were now operational, each with Satcom gear that could hook them directly into airborne command and control units, making Apache redundant. Having Apache's two helos handy were nice if they got into trouble—but only if the helos had enough gas to operate. Which couldn't happen without C-130s.

Besides, the plan called for a full squadron of AH-6s, with AC-130 gunships and four A-10s. That was the sort of firepower that made the risk worthwhile.

Wasn't going to happen. Better to leave Apache before it was discovered. It might come in handy during the ground war, assuming there was a ground war.

Hawkins sighed and took a long sip from his tea. He expected the order to bug out would come in a few hours. He and his men would be reassigned, most likely. Hopefully they'd end up doing something more important than playing palace guard for the bigwigs.

The captain took a last gulp of tea and met Doberman as he came down the ladder of the plane. "Nice landing," he told him.

"Yeah," answered the pilot. "Fucking short runway."

Hawkins wasn't sure exactly how to take that, so he ignored it. "I have two teams about a hundred miles north," Hawkins told him. "Both have laser designators."

"Yeah, well, those are useless as shit," said Doberman. He came to Hawkins's chest, but his voice was as deep as if he were six-eight.

To say nothing of his attitude.

"What do you mean?" the captain asked.

"I mean we have nothing to drop on what they point to," said Doberman. "You can have your fuel back, with a little interest. Where the fuck's Shotgun?"

Hawkins cocked his head to one side, his teeth edging against his lips. "He went out with one of my men to set up an observation post."

Doberman shook his head. "Fuck it."

"You got a problem, Captain?" asked Hawkins.

The pilot jerked his head up. "In what sense?"

Hawkins squinted his eyes at the shorter man, trying to figure him out. Doberman seemed to be one of those guys who went through life with a chip on his shoulder—or at least he came across that way.

As well as cocky and more than a bit arrogant.

While it was true that they were the same rank, Hawkins was in charge of the mission and the Hogs were assigned to work with him—or at least not against him. The pilot ought at least to make a stab at courtesy. But before he could deliver the overdue etiquette lecture, Hawkins spotted a suspicious cloud of dust rising northwest of the base.

He ran to a sandbagged position a few yards off the concrete, grabbing the binoculars that had been laid at the top of the low wall.

His FAV. Followed by an Iraqi tanker truck.

What the hell?

Hawkins watched as the two vehicles twisted across the scrubby sand toward him. Coors was hanging out the window of the tanker; the FAV was being driven by Shotgun. By the time they pulled onto the runway, everyone at Fort Apache not manning a lookout post had gathered to see what the hell was going on.

"Captain Hawkins, sorry we're a little late for tea," said Sergeant Coors, jumping from the truck with a grin.

"What is this, Coors?"

"We brought you some milk for your tea," answered Shotgun, unfolding himself from the FAV's driver's cage.

Hawkins listened as his sergeant explained what had happened. He was shaking his head vehemently before Coors got halfway through.

"What the hell were you thinking?" he demanded. "You should have come back here."

"I figured if there was someone in the truck, he would see the airplane when it took off or came back," said the sergeant. "I thought I'd have to do something quick."

"Which was what? Get lucky and nail him?"

"Hey, luck had nothing to do with it," said Shotgun.

"You're starting to bother me, Captain," snapped Hawkins. "Somebody go get a tarp to cover the back of this truck. Coors—you get a shovel and you start digging. I want this thing in the dirt. Did you cover your tracks off the road?"

"Jesus, I'm not stupid, sir," said Coors.

"Well, you sure as hell acted like it," said Hawkins.

The sergeant nailed his eyes to the ground in contrition. Not Shotgun.

"Milk's on the house," he said, opening the spigot control at the back of the truck. "Ought to just pour out of this thing here."

Captain Wong put his hand on his shoulder to stop him from taking a drink.

"In all likelihood, the tank was not properly decontaminated before it was filled," said Wong. "I believe you'll discover a proportion of distillate in the liquid, as well as a great deal of water."

"Ah, don't cry over spilt milk." Shotgun put his mouth beneath the spigot as he started the flow. He gagged and jumped back. "Wow. That's worse than Dogman's socks. Why didn't they clean the tank out right?"

"Because the truck's cargo isn't milk," said Captain Wong.

Hawkins watched him walk around the tanker, searching for something. Wong waved his hands over the shiny metal surface of the tanker, as if he were a faith healer. Finally, he stopped.

"Sergeant Rosen, would you happen to have an acetylene torch handy?" he asked.

The Air Force technical sergeant shook her head. "Sorry, no."

"The difficulties of operating in contingent circumstances." Wong sighed. "We'll have to drain the tank."

Hawkins had met Wong on a clandestine mission in

North Korea two years before; while eccentric, the intel officer was probably among the smartest and bravest guys in the service—certainly in the Air Force, a branch rapidly sinking in Hawkins's estimation. But it was often hard to tell what the hell he was up to.

"You wouldn't want to drink this," Wong told Hawkins as he opened the spigot at the rear and began draining the liquid. "Believe me."

"No shit."

Wong nodded.

"You going to explain what's going on, Bristol?" Hawkins asked. "Because I'll be damned if I can make sense of what the hell you're doing."

"There will be a compartment at the bottom of the tank, with bladders inside. We can get into it through the manhole once the liquid is removed. There isn't much."

"What are we looking for?"

Wong glanced over at the men, then back at Hawkins. He frowned as the liquid continued to flow but said nothing.

Hawkins finally guessed what Wong suspected.

"Coors, go get NBC gear on," he told his sergeant. "You're going to personally get to the bottom of this."

"It would be best for everyone to be prepared," Wong said to him. "And if Sergeant Coors is going inside the tank, a second suit over his primary gear would be optimum."

11

It wasn't until he became a squadron commander that Skull truly appreciated how hard enlisted personnel worked. Not all the time, of course; just when it mattered. He'd given lip service to the clichés about NCOs being the backbone of the Air Force, owing his life to crewdogs, etc., etc., but he hadn't really understood how true the sayings were until the first time he'd been responsible for getting a squadron of F-4 Phantoms in the air.

Partly that was because his first command was so badly screwed up when he arrived. The pilots were mediocre, but the real problem was the planes. The maintenance people were poorly trained, disorganized, and dispirited. And they stayed that way for exactly five days—which was how long it took him to get Clyston and a few other key NCOs over to his team. He called his guys the Mafia, and together they kicked enough butt to make their squadron one of the best in the Air Force—his bosses' opinion, not just his.

Most of the Mafia had long since retired, except for Clyston. But the new kids who came along to replace them were every bit as good, maybe better; if not smarter, they were more thoroughly trained and worked with better systems. Standing in the middle of the maintenance area—aka "Oz"—Skull marveled as his people overhauled the tail fin of a battle-damaged Hog; in the space of maybe twenty minutes, they had the plane stripped and reskinned.

"A little slow today," growled Clyston, winking at Skull as he passed to inspect the crew's handiwork. The colonel waited for the capo's well-rehearsed grunts to change to grudging approval before stepping forward himself to tell the men what a kick-butt job they were doing.

"And I *mean* kick-butt job," Knowlington repeated, aware that his voice was a little loud and a little shaky. "This is damn good work."

"All right, you heard the colonel," barked the capo. "Everybody take ten. You deserve it. Then I want that flap on six checked out. Let's go, let's go! Come on. Don't you guys know how to take a break, or do I have to send you back to school for that, too? Jee-zus-f'in' hell!"

Clyston grinned at Knowlington as the men scattered.

"You're getting a little predictable in your old age," Skull told him.

"Yeah, but they love it." The sergeant put his hands on his hips and snorted, laughing at himself.

"How are the men reacting to what happened to Dixon?" Skull asked.

"Well, I wouldn't say they're pleased." Clyston rolled his arms together at his chest. "But we'll get on. He hadn't been with most of these guys too long. And it wasn't one of our missions. That makes a difference."

Skull nodded. Clyston's cold assessment was undoubtedly correct. War's inevitable hardening process was well under way.

"How are you taking it?" the sergeant asked.

"Oh, like a wimp." Skull laughed. Clyston didn't. The colonel rubbed his neck and realized he hadn't shaved this morning, an odd thing to forget. "I hate losing kids, Allen. Especially like this."

"Sucks," said the sergeant.

More than two decades had passed since he'd met Clyston. He was an E-5 or E-3 or maybe even an airman then, crewing on butter-bar-nugget Michael Knowlington's "Thud," an F-105 Republic Thunderchief. They said hello and shared a cigarette—one of only two Knowlington ever smoked in his life—shortly before the green lieutenant climbed into the cockpit. Within the hour, Knowlington had dropped his first bombs and gotten his first air-to-air kill.

On that very same mission, a lieutenant who had flown with Knowlington back in the States went down over Laos. He was the first of many.

Vietnam had been a damn stupid war. But Knowlington didn't know that then. He didn't think it was a smart war, particularly, but he did think it was necessary. He figured he was sweating his fanny for something important, something like democracy and freedom, as corny as that sounded.

He still thought that. Mostly. But Vietnam had turned out to be a damn stupid war. Maybe this one would turn out the same way. It hadn't started all that smart.

"Colonel? You want some coffee or something?"

Skull snapped his head up, realizing his face was being scrutinized by the capo.

It was more than that. Skull realized he smelled of the Depot, its smoke and its booze.

He resisted the urge to tell the sergeant he was still sober—it would come off phony, make it seem like exactly the opposite was true.

"Thanks anyway," Knowlington said instead. "I'm about to start jittering with all the caffeine I've had already. I have a bunch of things to take care of back at the office. I just wanted to make sure you hadn't bitten off any heads today."

"None that didn't need biting."

Knowlington nodded.

"We're open twenty-four hours a day, seven days a week," said Clyston. "For any reason."

"I appreciate that, Allen. I appreciate it a lot," he told his old friend before walking away.

12

Rosen volunteered to go inside the tanker when it became obvious Coors wouldn't fit through the manhole without vast amounts of butter. Doberman couldn't object, not really—it was pretty clear they had to find out what the hell was inside the tanker and she was the only one who could get in and out. Still, he made them tie a rope around her so she could be hauled out in case something happened.

Alien bugs looked more humanlike than the small tech sergeant, who eased feet first into the black hole with a pair of tiny Special Ops flashlights in each hand. Doberman's heart pounded harder than it ever had—harder than when he'd been chased by the SAM, harder than his first solo. This was worse than flying, a hell of a lot worse. Flying, he could do something. When you were driving a Hog, or piloting any plane for that matter, there was a checklist. You did A, then you did B, then you did C. When you hit shit, you just moved through the list faster. But this—all he could do was watch.

He was seriously hooked on Rosen, he knew that. And the fact that he couldn't do anything about it up here was almost as hard to take as standing by helplessly as she disappeared inside the tanker.

The Hog pilots were wearing special NBC underwear beneath their flightsuits and theoretically could have gotten by with booties, gloves, and headgear, but both Doberman and Shotgun donned full suits borrowed from the commandos. He couldn't see all that well through the hood's small visor, and he was tempted to whip it off as Rosen emerged with what looked like an oversized purse. Wong, next to her on top of the back of the truck, took it and threw it to the ground. She returned twice more with two more purses.

Doberman walked around to the back of the truck to look at them. He got about five feet away before Wong jumped in front of him, waving his hands like a flagman waving off traffic. Doberman cursed but stopped, watching as Wong poked the bags with a wand from a small device the commando team had supplied. He prodded and nudged for about ten minutes before straightening. He gestured for Rosen to stay near the bags, then walked back to Hawkins.

"The bags are empty. The seals were never implemented," said Wong after lifting the hood off his head.

Wong had to be the only guy in the Air Force who actually looked natural in the chem suit. The bulky gear made his head seem almost normal-sized.

"What does that mean?" Hawkins asked.

"These weren't used. This device is primitive," he added, holding up the meter in his hands, "but it should be sufficient to detect traces of most toxins the Iraqis might use. It's clean. But we should wrap the bags according to full protocol. We should also proceed as if the tanker itself was contaminated."

"Why?" Doberman asked.

Wong frowned, as he always did when asked to explain. He held out his gloved hand and counted the points. "One: the Iraqis are not renowned for their safety precautions. Two: the bags were in the open compartment, absurdly foolish, even for the Iraqis. Three: the tanker was oriented in a western direction. Four—"

"What does the fact that it was going west have to do with anything?" asked Doberman.

"I surmise that it was returning rather than arriving at its destination," said Wong.

"You're telling me that it delivered chemicals somewhere?" said Hawkins.

"That would be a leap in logic that I am not prepared to make, especially since we are speaking about the Iraqis," said Wong. "But it would be foolish not to consider that a distinct possibility. The most likely theory is that these bags were never filled. Rather, they accompanied similar bags, which have now been deposited at some destination further west."

"Maybe they were on their way to get filled," said Shotgun.

"Admittedly a possibility," said Wong. "I would note, however, that the temperature of the liquid they were submerged in was the same as the truck, which suggests the liquid had been in the truck a long time. Such would be the case certainly if the truck were making its way back after a morning delivery, but not if it had only just taken on the milk in preparation for its mission."

"What do we now?" asked Hawkins.

"I suggest we examine the map your sergeant discovered and see where the truck has been," said Wong. "And then we attempt to act on that information."

"I knew we'd get around to blowing something up eventually," said Shotgun.

The Iraqis were not so cooperative as to have marked their drop-off with an *X,* but Wong worked over the map like a forensic scientist—or, as Shotgun put it, a witch doctor summoning the dead. He claimed that the folds and pen impressions in the paper showed that the truck had followed a course from near or in Jordan west, into some hills about fifteen miles from Sugar Mountain, where Doberman and Shotgun had blown up a storage bunker that morning.

Had it stopped at the bunker? Wong couldn't say. Had it made a delivery or picked something up there? Wong couldn't say. What had it done afterward? Wong couldn't say.

And somehow, everybody nodded and called him a genius.

Doberman nodded as Hawkins said he would authorize a recon mission to the village where the truck had apparently turned around. Called Al-Kajuk on the map, none of the Delta teams Scud hunting up north were close enough to check it out; Fort Apache would have to send its own people.

"There are three or four buildings large enough to be storage facilities there," Hawkins told Wong as they examined the maps and some satellite photos near the truck. "It's pretty close to Sugar Mountain. Maybe the buildings there house Scuds."

"The facility at Sugar Mountain may well be related," said Wong. "They might have kept the chemicals there, then moved them with this or another vehicle. Or it could be a co-incidence. It could conceivably be a decoy."

"Doubt it," said Hawkins.

"So this could be a wild-goose chase," said Doberman. It seemed to him they were jumping to way too many conclusions here.

Hawkins glared at him. The Army guy definitely had a stick up his butt, Doberman decided.

Tall guys always did.

"If it's a wild-goose chase," said Hawkins sharply, "it's my wild-goose chase."

"Not if we're giving you air cover," said Doberman.

"Bullshit."

"What do you mean bullshit?" said Doberman. "What the hell do you think we're doing here?"

"One of your planes is still grounded," said the Delta Force captain. "And as for you—"

"Captain O'Rourke's plane is good to go," announced Rosen, joining the small group huddled in Hawkins's command post.

"You found a patch?" asked Shotgun.

"I borrowed a few things from the tanker truck. I don't think the Iraqis will be needing brakes anytime soon, do you? Or clamps?"

"Will the patch hold?" Doberman asked her.

"As long as he doesn't stop for candy. I even got the pressure up, borrowing off fluid from the other, uh, I made it work." Something caught in her throat as they looked at each other. Rosen's face flushed and then became very serious. "Yes, sir, I think it will."

Sir?

Why had her face flushed?

"We don't need air cover. I have my helos," said Hawkins. "Thanks for the report, Sergeant."

"I thought you were low of fuel," said Doberman.

"I'll make do."

"Here's what I'm thinking," said Shotgun. "Dog Man and me ride out there and see what's going on. We find something moving, we shoot it up. We don't, you guys sneak in at night."

"We can't wait for night," said Hawkins. "We have to be out of here by then."

"You're bugging out?" said Doberman.

"That's right, Captain. If it's okay with you."

"So why are we having this discussion?"

"We are not having this discussion," said Hawkins. "I am talking about the situation with Captain Wong."

"Wong works for me," said Doberman.

"Begging your pardon," said Wong, who was crossing his legs like he was standing on a ten-hour pee, "but in fact I am assigned to Admiral—"

"Yeah, yeah, my point is, why are we wasting our time talking about this if you guys are going home?" said Doberman.

"Because there's plenty of time to check this out in the meantime," said Hawkins. "We're not leaving until nightfall. This is a potential Scud site with chemical warheads."

"So is every damn town in Iraq, by your criteria," said Doberman. "You just want to play Rambo."

"You're out of line, Captain," roared Hawkins.

"Hey, Dog Man, time for a walk," said Shotgun, grabbing Doberman by the arm before he could respond with a roar of his own. His wingman picked him up by the arms and carried him fifty yards into the desert before finally letting go.

"Damn it, Shotgun. Let the hell go of me."

"You're out of line, Dog. Way out of line. Those guys saved our butts."

Shotgun's voice had a tone to it so rare that Doberman felt as if he'd been slapped across the face. His throat thickened as he lowered his voice, managing to calm his tone if not all his anger.

"That doesn't mean we can let them go off and get themselves greased on a wild-goose chase," said Doberman.

"Wong thinks it's worth taking a look."

"Wong."

"Braniac's an expert, Dog Man. Besides, what the hell do you think these Delta guys were sent up here for? They're in the wild-goose-chasing business, don't you think? That's half the fun of Spec Ops."

"Yeah, fun. This isn't a game, Gun. We lost a squadron mate today."

"I know that." Shotgun gave him a disapproving frown. "But we got a job to do. I agree with you, we go where they go. But we have to play it their way."

"I hate it when you get serious, Shotgun," Doberman said. "You're a lot more fun joking around."

"That's what I'm talking about."

"Yeah. All right. Shit." Doberman stamped his feet against the ground. "We ought to be the ones to check out the village."

"If we do that, we're going to have to get real close and personal, which'll definitely tip them off. Think about it," said Shotgun. "We can't stand back with Mavericks and play push-button bye-bye. No sir. If we only have the cannons to take them out, it'd be better to know what we were shooting at before we went in. I mean, I like dodging flak as much as anybody, but it sure helps to know where you're going when you're duckin'." Shotgun's voice had gradually resumed its normal bounce, and now the desert practically shook with its overstated, but for Shotgun routine, enthusiasm. "What we ought to do is have the Delta boys go in there, scout the area, then call us in once they have a target. This way we're just in and out, no fooling around. That's what I'm talking about. No muss, lots of fuss."

"Yeah," said Doberman. "Fucker was holding out on us with the fuel. I could have been killed."

"Nah. He's just blowing his reserves now because they're leaving," said Shotgun. "Besides, you're too damn lucky to get killed."

"Right."

"It's what I'm talking about."

He still wasn't convinced, but there was nothing to do about it now. "You think Rosen's fix on the hydraulic line'll hold?" Doberman asked.

"Ah, there's two different lines, for cryin' out loud. Hey, I can fly the Hog without hydraulics. Jeez, plane and me been flying together so long I can steer her on thought power if I have to. Now, what I'm worried about is finding some decent coffee. Have you tasted the stuff they're trying to pass off as joe up here? My aunt brews better stuff for her cat. And she hates her cat." Shotgun shook his head sadly. "Was a time being a Delta *operator* meant you were skilled in basic survival skills. Standards are going right down the poop chute. That's what I'm talking about."

13

Finally lashed into his F-15C Eagle cockpit with his seat restraints cinched, Major Horace "Hack" Preston gave his crew chief a thumbs-up. The sergeant nodded, then reached over and removed the last safety pin from the ejector seat before disappearing down the boarding ladder. Hack said his customary prayer and turned his eyes to his kneepad. He'd already memorized nearly all of the details of his mission—he'd been blessed with a nearly photographic memory—but repeating each bit of flight data aloud had become an important part of the preflight ritual, and he'd sooner have left his zipper suit back in the barn than take off without flipping through the neat rows of carefully lettered notes. Navigation points, frequencies, tanker tracks, even some weather notes filled the small pages on the pad. Hack worked through quickly but methodically, thumbing his way to the board at the bottom. The thin piece of wood had flown with him now for nearly five years. The top half contained two sayings. Hack dutifully read and recited both to himself:

> Wisdom excelleth folly,
> as far as light excelleth darkness.
>
> Do your best.

The first saying was from Ecclesiastes in the Bible. The second he had heard from his father nearly every day until leaving for the Air Force Academy.

Beneath the words was a Gary Larson cartoon about an entomologist. There was no reason, really, for the cartoon, except that it had once struck him as hilarious. He looked at it, smiled, and flicked the paper back in place, completing his routine.

The cartoon was the only frivolous thing in the gleaming F-15 Eagle, unarguably the most potent operational interceptor in the world, and—to Hack and his squadron mates, certainly—the star of the Gulf War.

Ready for his mission, Hack waited while the huffer—a diesel-powered device on a large mobile cart used by the ground crew to start the plane's engine—kicked the fighter's F100-PW-200 turbofans to life. Hack allowed himself a moment to soak in the rumble, then proceeded through his pretakeoff checklist, slowly but surely making sure the plane was ready to go.

While the interceptor could be quickly scrambled into action, under normal circumstances the preflight briefings and prep work stretched past two hours—sometimes twice as long as the "working" portion of the mission. Hack's especially—he was notorious for demanding a high level of preparation before the Eagles under his command took to the sky. Better to take care of a problem on the ground, he figured, than at thirty thousand feet.

Piranha Flight's four interceptors were slated to patrol a wide swatch of western Iraq this afternoon, working in pairs as roving marshals on the Wild Western frontier. Their missions had become progressively more aggressive and freewheeling as the air war proceeded. While other Eagles and Coalition fighters might be part of large packages of planes with specific flights to escort, the Piranhas had been tasked today as roving interceptors. Working with a controller in an AWACS E-3 Sentry, Hack and his flight would fly in a long loop or racetrack high over enemy territory. At the first sign of activity, they would be vectored in for a kill.

While the Piranhas had flown several such missions already, they had yet to fire in anger. Today, however, promised to be different—for the first time, their track would take them near a large enemy air base. It housed at least a dozen MiGs and its runway had survived numerous bombings by the British RAF. The intelligence specialists at Black Hole reported that the Iraqis were getting anxious; a U-2 spy plane had caught support vehicles moving around the ground. Word was, the Iraqi planes were going to try and make a run for it, maybe to Iran.

Which pleased Hack no end. His mission—his job, his life—was to splash MiGs. He hoped and had even prayed last night that he would have a chance to do so today.

He'd also prayed that he wouldn't screw up.

Hack snapped the mike button and requested clearance from ground control. Acknowledged and approved, he slipped the Eagle's throttles out of idle and nudged from his parking spot.

Hack hated this part of the flight—his stomach stirred with anticipation, juices building. Inevitably, he poked the stick around like a novice, shaking the plane's control surfaces like a new lieutenant queuing for his first flight.

"Tower, Piranha One, in sequence," he began, asking the controller for his departure ticket.

"Piranha, the wind three-two-zero at twelve knots, cleared for takeoff."

"Piranha," he acknowledged, leading the rest of his flight toward the long gray splash of runway where they would take off. His stomach jerked back and forth furiously, climbing up his windpipe as he glanced through the large bubble canopy at his wingman Captain "Johnny" Stern. Stern gave him a thumbs-up; he returned it, then got serious, poking his Pratt & Whitneys to full military power while checking his instruments. RPM, turbine inlet temp, oil pressure, and fuel flow were at spec. He checked them off in his head, working quickly through the numbers for engine two. His stomach boiled—the temp gauge for the inlet read 322 degrees Celsius, about 900 Fahrenheit, and he might have believed that was measuring his own temperature.

Do your best.

When the brakes were released, the Eagle didn't roll down the runway—it bolted, pushing itself against his back as it jumped from zero to 120 knots in nothing flat. Hack went to takeoff power and brought the stick back steadily. The F-15 could literally fly straight up off the runway, but there was no need to show off. The Eagle lifted herself into the desert air, past the fine mist of sand, beyond the heated air radiating in waves off the concrete. The fire in his stomach subsided; he settled into the routine, cleaning up the airplane by cranking in the wheels and adjusting his flaps. The Eagle was already moving through the air at over 220 nautical miles an hour. As the unsafe gear lights blinked off, Hack checked through his instruments, making sure he was in the green. Then he swept his head around the cockpit glass nearly three hundred degrees, from one end of the ejector seat cushion to the other, back to front to back, before beginning a bank to set course to the flight's rendezvous point.

Once the flight was airborne, the four Eagles split into two sections. Hack and his wingmate went north; the second group stayed south, queuing up to tank. They would trade places in roughly forty-five minutes, one group in reserve while the other zipped over southwestern Iraq at roughly twenty-five thousand feet.

Hack and his wingman were just falling into their first sweep when the AWACS broke the loud hush in his ears with the words he'd prayed to hear.

"Boogies coming off the runway at H-2."

Oh yeah, thought Hack. *Oh yeah.*

14

Shotgun adjusted the harness on his seat restraint, rocked back and forth, and played with the rudder pedals as he sat off to the side of the Apache runway, waiting for Doberman to clear so he could trundle into takeoff position. His Hog had been fueled, he had close to a full combat load in the Gatling-style cannon beneath his chair, and the plane had just been given a personal going-over by the best A-10A maintenance tech this side of the capo di capo.

Still, he couldn't help feeling a little discombobulated.

Not anxious, exactly, not worried or nervous—those words weren't in his vocabulary, at least not as they pertained to flying. Just *off.*

Discombobulated.

Part of it was that, to conserve fuel, the Warthog was going to be pushed to the far end of the runway. Not that it made that much difference to him, but the plane was apt to feel embarrassed, especially with all these Spec Ops guys watching. In Shotgun's opinion, the eleven seconds or so of flight time that would be gained weren't worth the indignity, but Doberman was in such an obviously bad mood today that Shotgun had just nodded when he suggested that.

But the real trouble wasn't the Hog's ego. He was flying without his proper load of equipment. Not having Mavericks or iron bombs was bad enough, but going to war without candy or treats—that was truly a hardship.

Actually, he did have one Twinkie, wrapped in its protective plastic covering in his flightsuit. He eyed its bulge in his shin pocket longingly, aching to taste its luscious yellow flesh and creamy white arteries, but not wanting to be without hope of sustenance at a critical moment in battle.

War was hell, but this was the kind of thing that made him mad. Not to mention hungry.

Shotgun was aware that most combat pilots, perhaps even all combat pilots, never ate on the job. There was all the flight gear to deal with—the mask, the helmet, the pressure suit. There was gravity and there were altitude effects which played havoc with your taste buds. And admittedly, the wrong crumb in the navigational gear could send you to Beijing instead of Baghdad, though he figured that was the sort of mistake you had to make the most of.

But Shotgun wasn't another combat pilot; he was a Hog driver, and Hog drivers were genetically equipped to do the impossible. He had stuffed a Tootsie Roll in his mouth on his very first flight in an A-10A, savoring the chewy chocolate flavor through his first roll. The next day he had discovered that few things in the world could compare with the shock of three or four g's hitting you square in the esophagus as you bit down on a Drake's cherry pie. It made the blood race; it made you feel like you were an American, connected to the great unbroken chain of 7-Elevens strung across the Heartland. It was what he was fighting for.

Out on the runway, Doberman lit his twin turbofans. Unlike many other planes, the Hogs were equipped with on-board starters that allowed them to operate at scratch bases like these; they were just one of the many features that made the A-10 the ultimate do-it-yourself airplane. Doberman's mount jerked forward quickly, pulling herself in the sky two hundred feet before the wadi.

Rosen ran in front of Shotgun's Hog and gave him a thumbs-up. The pilot released the brakes and the soldiers began pushing the plane forward. He could tell the Hog didn't like this—she grunted and creaked, dragging her tail across the concrete like a dog yelled at for peeing on the rug.

"Get over it," he barked at the Hog. She stopped her whining, rolling freely and poking her tail surfaces around as Shotgun pedaled her into the wind.

Rosen's fixes to the hydraulic system couldn't be properly tested until he was in the air. Under other circumstances, the checkflight would have been conducted very carefully, according to a rigidly prescribed to-do list. Here, though, Shotgun was basically going to make sure everything worked on the fly.

Which suited him just fine. He'd never been much of a test pilot. Too many questions to answer.

He lit the GE TF34-GE-100 turbofans on the back hull. The Hog roared her approval, bucking her nose up and down. Brakes off, she began striding down the short run of concrete, willing herself off the ground. Shotgun had the wheels coming up as she thundered over the dark crease at the runway's end. She gave a wag of her tail to the men still working to bury the tanker, as if she were saying good-bye to the organ donor who'd helped her carry on. Shotgun brought her to course, cranked "Born to Run"—kind of mandatory, when you thought about it—and reached for his customary post-takeoff Twizzler.

And came up empty.

Discombobulated.

"Now I'm starting to really get pissed off," he said, sweeping his eyes across his readouts. Speed brisk, compass doing its thing, altitude moving in the proper direction. The master caution on the warning panel—no light, good. Enunciators clean, good.

With only the Sidewinder missiles and ECM pod under her wings, the Hog felt clean and light, and gave no hint that she was flying with a patched hydraulic system. Rosen's fix had held.

"Devil One, this is Two," Shotgun said over the squadron frequency, contacting Doberman as he set course in a loose trail roughly three miles behind his flight leader. Their initial direction was south, toward open desert, where it was unlikely they'd be spotted as they climbed. They would then fly northeast toward Kajuk, where the Delta patrol was due to be arriving any second now. "I'm up."

"About time," grunted Doberman.

"You get the helos on the air yet?"

"They're in the green. Team's on the ground," Doberman told him. "They should be ready for us in fifteen minutes."

"My math has us over the target in ten," said Shotgun, who actually was just guessing. He hadn't been very big on math since Sister Harvey's class in fifth grade.

"Yeah, twelve," said Doberman. "Conserve your fuel."

"I go any slower I'm walking," Shotgun told him. "I'm surprised you can hear me over the stall warnings."

"One," snapped Doberman, an acknowledgment that basically meant shut up and drive.

Captain Wong had gone along with the Delta team to make sure things worked right; with Braniac on the job, Shotgun figured they'd have no problem finding a target. They had maybe twenty minutes' worth of fuel to spend circling south of the target area before they'd have to head back to Al-Jouf.

Ten, according to Doberman, but the flight leader liked to pad those calculations.

Doberman's tail was a small black line in the upper left quadrant of Shotgun's windshield. The loose trail formation was a *de rigueur* Hog lineup for a two-plane element. It was basically follow-the-leader with a slight offset; the trail plane flew behind the leader's right or left wing, back anywhere from a half mile to three, depending on the circumstances. The planes would generally fly at slightly different altitudes, making it a little more difficult for an approaching enemy to pick out both in one glance. Freelancing attack gigs like this sortie and the others typically flown by Hogs tended to be somewhat less precise than the carefully orchestrated plans employed by vast packages of advanced bombers and escorts, since flexibility was generally the key to success. The overall pattern was always the same, though: the wingman protected the lead plane's six. Depending on the target, the planes would fall into a quick, two-fisted ground attack or a more leisurely figure-eight wheel-and-dive, each looking out for the other.

"How's that repair holding up?" Doberman asked.

"Fine," Shotgun replied. "I'm dyin' up here, though. Nothing to eat."

"You didn't check the seat for crumbs?"

"Now that you mention it, there's probably a gumdrop or two under the sofa."

Shotgun was just considering whether he might really have dropped something under one of the panels when the plane jerked left.

He knew by the feel even as he muscled his stick that it wasn't the hydraulics. He'd lost power in his right engine.

Gone. Dead. Dormant.

What the hell?

Shotgun worked through the restart procedure, thought he had a cough.

Nada. He tried twice more and came up empty.

Serious caution lights; the damn cockpit looked like a Christmas tree.

Well, all right, a slight exaggeration. But this is what came of flying without even a good-luck Three Musketeers bar.

Shotgun cast his eyes toward his last resort—the lone Twinkie. Then he snapped the mike button in disgust.

"Devil One, this is Two. I've got a situation."

15

Three weeks ago to the day, Bristol Wong had been enjoying a leisurely game of chess in a small club frequented by Pentagon and CIA intelligence specialists in Alexandria, Virginia. With its thick leather chairs, horse paintings, and frankly British decor, the club appealed to the Air Force captain's innate sense of culture and decorum. The fact that a good game of chess and reasonably decent sherry could always be had there didn't hurt. But on that very day, Wong had no sooner settled into a Sicilian defense—old hat to be sure, but he was playing a former CIA agent well known for his love of extreme symmetry—when his beeper vibrated. Wong knew instantly that he was going to hate the next four or five weeks of his life.

An hour after returning the call, Wong found himself aboard a Navy transport plane, en route to Saudi Arabia, armed with a title several sentences long that had little to do with his actual mission. Officially, his job was to "consult and brief" Centcom on Iraqi air defenses; his actual task was to gather information about any and all advanced Soviet systems in the theater, which would be provided backchannel to the Pentagon G2's chief of staff. The dual nature of his mission was nothing particularly out of the ordinary, at least not for Wong, who was, after all, the world's greatest expert on Russian weapons—outside the Soviet Union, of course.

In due course, he made his way to Hog Heaven and Devil Squadron at their Home Drome, also known as King Fahd Royal Air Base. He was chasing down a lead on the use of a shoulder-fired weapon that both the CIA and the Air Force claimed the Iraqis didn't possess—the SA-16, a relatively sophisticated shoulder-fired weapon in some ways comparable to an American Stinger. While publicly expressing skepticism with the report, Wong in fact already had ample evidence that the missile was in Iraqi possession, and suspected that they were even using an improved version only recently issued to Russian troops themselves. A member of Devil Squadron—Captain Glenon, in fact—had had the misfortune of encountering one during the first day of the war.

Unfortunately for Wong, the Devil Squadron commander—Colonel Michael Knowlington—took an inexplicable liking to him and managed to pull all manner of strings to have him assigned to his command. Naturally, Wong realized that he would be a prize jewel in any command structure, and had employed a vast array of tactics to get himself removed and returned to Washington, D.C., where he might play chess with some regularity, not to mention challenge.

But his efforts had been misinterpreted; Colonel Knowlington now considered him an essential cog in the machine, and detailed him to help the advance elements of Devil Squadron supporting Fort Apache.

Which was how he found himself here, close to two hundred miles inside Iraq, sucking dirt as the interminable wind whipped up through the hills surrounding the small pimple of a settlement called Al-Kajuk. He and the Delta troopers accompanying him had at least a mile of climbing to do before getting a clear view of the village, such as it was.

Wong had worked with Delta and other Spec Ops troops before. Aside from a predilection for running when walking would have been sufficient, he found them competent, professional, and taciturn, characteristics he thoroughly appreciated.

The sergeant in front of him held up a hand, signaling a stop. Wong passed the signal along to the team's com specialist behind him, who in turn passed it on to the tail gunner. There were only four troopers on this ad hoc team: Sergeant Mays at point, Sergeant Franks at the rear, Sergeant Holgrum with the satellite communications gear, and Sergeant Golden, the team leader. Golden was in charge; Wong was in theory just along as an advisor, and knew better than to interfere.

"Let's rest here a minute," said Golden, coming back. "We have a house or something over that hump and down the slope, maybe half a mile, a little more. That way there's a road and the village, and over there's the highway, on our right. Looks like we get to the peak, we'll be exposed, sun in our faces. We should be able to position the Satcom up there somewhere, but let's scout the area first. Kind of weird we got vegetation that side of the hill and pretty much nothing here," he added. "Must be water underground or something."

Wong nodded. He suspected that the vegetation on the long, sloping hillside to their left had more to do with the wind pattern, which would amplify the modest moisture effect produced by the nearby river, but he knew from experience that meteorological matters hardly ever interested anyone, except while waiting for a train.

"Captain Wong and I will go on ahead," the sergeant told the others. "That okay with you, Captain?"

"It would suit me." Wong dropped his pack on the ground, pulling his M-16A and its 203 grenade launcher up under his arm. It was not his preferred weapon, but would serve.

"Captain Hawkins said you were with him when he jumped into Korea," said Golden. The sergeant was short for a Green Beret, about five-eight, and fairly skinny. Wong, at six-two, towered over him, even on the incline.

"Yes. An interesting mission."

"You killed two gooks?"

Wong smiled at the racial slur, but didn't answer. Golden was white, but obviously of mixed ancestry; no one ethnic group could have produced a face quite so ugly. Wong himself was fifth-generation British-Chinese-American, born in Hong Kong to a Scottish mother—not quite classic "gook," but undoubtedly close enough for the sergeant.

"We may be doing some killing here," said Golden. "I know you Pentagon boys don't like to get your hands dirty."

"I would not be surprised to find mine are dirtier than yours," Wong said, starting up the hill ahead of him.

16

Doberman eyeballed the paper map on his kneeboard as Shotgun gave his wayward engine another shot at relighting itself. He had already decided he was sending his wingmate home, no matter what, but he realized the news wasn't going to go over very well.

"Damn, Dog Breath, she won't catch for me no way, no how," cursed Shotgun. "Son of a bitch."

"Yeah, okay, you think you can make Al-Jouf?"

"You sending me home without supper?"

"You have to go back, Shotgun."

"Yeah, I know, I know. Damn. You ever, ever heard of one of these engines giving out? Ever?"

There was only one acceptable response. "No. Must be a fluke," said Doberman. "All right, let's go."

"I don't need you holding my hand," answered Shotgun.

"The most important thing is that you get back in one piece. I have a course laid out."

That unleashed a stream of curses loud enough to nearly shatter Doberman's shatterproof helmet.

Flying solo with one engine—frankly, even with two—over hostile territory was not exactly risk-free, but Shotgun pointed out that Doberman had a job to do. There were plenty of Coalition aircraft to call on if needed. Besides, there were worse things than flying on one engine, especially as far as he was concerned.

"See now, this is the kind of thing that really pisses me off," said Shotgun, his tirade trickling down. "This Delta coffee tastes like green tea."

Doberman nudged his stick, widening the circle he was drawing over the Iraqi scrubland. Al-Kajuk lay ten miles to the northeast. Iraqi air defenses were thin but still potent, and the village could easily be hiding flak guns and mobile missiles. He was at eight thousand feet, circling high enough so he couldn't be heard, but the sky was clear and anyone with a good set of eyes, not to mention binoculars, ought to be able to spot him from the ground. And if a radar turned on, well, that was show business.

"If you think you can make it—" Doberman started.

"It's what I'm talking about. Hell. Unless you don't think you can handle things."

"Screw you," snapped Doberman.

"Anytime."

"Yeah, all right. Sorry about the coffee," Doberman told his wingmate.

"Coffee's the only reason I'm going to Al-Jouf," said Shotgun. "You want anything?"

"Taco with beans," Doberman answered.

"I'll see what I can do," said Shotgun. "Devil Two, gone. You're solo."

Shotgun had a million personal call signs, sign-offs, nicknames, curses, and slang sayings, but that was one Doberman had never heard before.

"Yeah," was all he could reply.

The Warthog's top speed was supposedly 439 miles an hour, though there was considerable debate and not a little bragging among Hog drivers about the "real" speed. It was a kind of inverse of bragging—pilots liked to say how slow the A-10A *really* flew, even going downhill with the wind at her back.

Normal cruising speed was less than four hundred miles an hour, so slow that a World War II–era propeller-driven fighter could easily keep up. Cutting his circles around the Iraqi desert south of his target area, Doberman's indicated airspeed was exactly 385 nautical miles an hour.

Vital flight data was projected in front of his eyes via a HUD or heads-up display. While it was easy to see out of the airplane, the front windshield area was narrow and even cluttered by the standards of planes like the F-15 or F-16. But it was also better protected. A thick frame held armored windscreen panels, a tacit acknowledgment of the fact that the people a Hog driver most wanted to meet weren't welcoming him with open arms. Doberman sat in what amounted to a bathtub constructed of titanium; the mass of metal protected the airplane's most vital part: him. If at times—like now—he felt like a bear in a cave, it was a highly secure cave.

The ground team, "Snake Eaters," was supposed to come on the air at precisely 1600, or in one minute and thirteen seconds. Doberman, impatient by nature, tried to divert himself by starting a very slow instrument check. He began with his fuel gauge, a large clock-faced dial over the right console, just above a selector switch that allowed him to separately measure the stores in the various tanks. He moved deliberately, slowly, precisely, expecting to be interrupted—hoping, actually—but concentrating on what he was doing.

There were two kinds of pilots, in Doberman's opinion: guys like Shotgun, who were really birds in disguise, equipped with some sort of sixth sense about planes. And there were guys like him, who had trained themselves essentially by rote and repetition. Doberman had an engineering background, and he thought like an engineer, or at least tried to, leaving nothing to chance. He calculated the fuel readings against his estimated time over target and reserves, running the numbers quickly through his mental computer to make sure he had all his contingencies covered. Then he walked his eyes over the rest of the readouts and instruments, temperatures, pressures, speed, altitude, heading. Check, check, check. Gun ready as she would ever be, threat indicator clean, check, check, check.

And where the hell was Wong and the rest of the ground team? It was already 1603.

He started to click his mike button to try and hail him when the AWACS controller cut in with a warning: enemy planes were coming off a runway less than fifty miles northeast of him.

17

At the precise moment Doberman was wondering what was going on below, Wong was holding his breath and sliding down between two very large and uncomfortable rocks ten feet from an Iraqi soldier.

Two soldiers, actually, though he had only a good idea where one of them was. Wong suspected there were even more manning the small guard post just beneath the summit of the hill.

Sergeant Golden crouched about six feet to his left, training his MP-5 in the Iraqis' direction. While Golden had a silenced version of the Heckler & Koch, "silence" was a relative term for submachine guns; the weapon would be heard by anyone nearby. The sergeant was therefore unsheathing his combat knife, hoping the guards would come close enough to be plucked.

One good thing—the Iraqis wouldn't be there if they didn't have an excellent view of the highway and village.

On the other hand, they probably wouldn't be there without some sort of radio.

Wong slid his hand into the back of his desert-chip fatigues, pulling out his own knife. Molded and tempered from titanium to his specifications, the weapon's blade was barely six inches long—150 mm to be precise. Honed like a barber's razor, the single-edged cutting blade was 45 mm at its widest point, shaped for what Wong had determined by careful study of several obscure medieval Korean texts was the best angle for severing the arteries of the neck and throat.

Medieval Korean was a job to translate, but the labor elicited a certain mental vigor difficult to duplicate. And nobody knew as much about knives as ancient Koreans, in his opinion.

Knife ready and eyes trained on the summit, Wong carefully worked a small grenade into his launcher so that the weapon would be ready to fire if needed. The gun was a breechloader, admirable in its simplicity—and liable to be set off accidentally or by the enemy once he put it down between the rocks, only semihidden. But the contingencies demanded a certain percentage of risk.

Golden looked at him. Wong removed the Beretta from his belt—a stock but nonetheless dependable weapon—and nodded. He understood that the sergeant intended on taking the man on the left whose foot was just now appearing at the top of the hill; he would take the man closest to him, whose footsteps were now conveniently approaching up the hill parallel to his comrade. Wong would attempt to take him silently with the knife, reserving the pistol.

Contrary to popular belief, most if not all elite troops considered the knife a weapon of absolute last resort. It exposed the user to an immense amount of danger and, no matter how good the weapon, represented the least potent force multiplier available. Wong ranked it far below his preferred options, which naturally started with ten-megaton nuclear warheads. Still, there was no denying the primal thrill a knife represented. The knife wielder joined a long string of ancients, a royalty that included the ancient slayer of Beowulf, a glorious slob of a man who rolled a thick blade into the belly of the archetypal beast.

Wong's aim was considerably higher as he sprang on the guard. His right hand jerked across the front of the Iraqi's throat as his left hand brought the butt end of his pistol hard against the soldier's skull. As the man coughed and began to fall Wong saw a third Iraqi four yards down the slope, turning toward him with a rifle in his hand. He drew his hand back and whipped the knife forward, striking the soldier in the throat with such force that he dropped his AK-47. Wong rushed forward before the man could recover, applying a kick to render him unconscious.

Technically speaking, the kick to the head was not particularly well executed; his karate master would have been appalled. But it did its job, incapacitating the Iraqi. Wong dropped to a knee, scanning the area with his handgun as he retrieved his knife.

"Damn good work with the ragheads," said Sergeant Golden between hard breaths. His man lay in the dirt a few yards away, skull broken and neck slashed.

"Ragheads is probably not technically correct," said Wong.

Golden began to laugh. "You're a pisser. Where'd you get that sense of humor, Wong?"

"The appellation 'raghead' would seem to be meant for nomadic tribesmen or, with less precision, to members of the Islamic faith," said Wong. "Neither of which any of these men were. For example, this man has a cross around his neck, and—"

"Jesus, Captain, you're a ballbuster," said Golden. "That's their radio."

As Wong surveyed the slope looking for other Iraqis, he wondered why everyone in Iraq seemed to think he was a comedian. The fact that the men were not Muslims was highly unusual and undoubtedly significant, though at the moment he wasn't sure what it might mean.

"I think we're clear," said the sergeant.

"I concur."

"You figure we can put the Satcom on the ridge?"

"Or just below," said Wong, gesturing over the hill. "In the meantime, if you lend me your glasses I will examine the village. I have a clear view."

"Gotcha."

A dozen small houses made of yellowish brick or cement nestled along a small road jutting against a shallow hillside. Two larger buildings sat along the only paved road, which led to the highway. Constructed of concrete block, they were perfectly suited as warehouses. Beyond the hill was a mosque. The paint on its minaret had faded somewhat, but the tower was impressive, out of proportion for the mosque itself and much newer.

Standing, Wong scanned down the road to the highway. He followed the highway several miles to the east. There were several fields with irrigation systems, though at the moment they did not seem to be under cultivation. In the distance, he could see more signs of population; houses and other buildings were scattered like pieces from a discarded Monopoly game.

The highway ran over a large culvert about three miles from the hill. A ramp had been dozed off the side, as if to prepare for a cloverleaf exit.

Or, much more likely, a Scud launching spot. The missiles could be placed beneath the roadway until ready for launch.

Golden set up the dish for the Satcom just behind the crest of the hill. It took a few minutes to position it properly; as they did, Wong studied the culvert.

"I have contact with the A-10s," said Golden. "They're waiting for a target."

"There's an erector hidden beneath the highway in that culvert," Wong told him, pointing out the shadow in the distance. He was just about to hand the glasses to the sergeant when he noticed a pickup truck and what seemed to be a large APC approaching on the highway. A brown tarp flapped loosely over the rear of the carrier. "Excuse me," he said, putting the glasses back to his eyes to examine the trucks.

He watched as they approached the culvert. He was not surprised to see them stop, but Wong at first wondered why the larger vehicle did not pull down under the roadway with the pickup.

And then he saw why.

"Hmmph," he said.

"What is it?" asked Golden.

"I have not seen SA-9s for some time now," admitted Wong. He watched a pair of Iraqis adjust the netting that helped camouflage the mobile missile launcher; the battery appeared ready for action. "Frankly, I had not considered that we might encounter them."

"Problem?" asked Golden.

"Problem is a relative word," said Wong, handing the sergeant the glasses. "But I would not describe this as a positive development."

18

Hack cursed, unable to sort out the bandits in the chaos. More than fifty contacts crowded into the F-15's powerful radar, and now he had another problem—the RWR warned that a ground radar had just popped to life north of him.

The Piranhas' radio frequency—in theory assigned only to them—jammed with talk from two other flights as Hack's brain began swimming with the black chaos of battle-induced stress. He flipped his radar back and forth through search modes, but couldn't get a positive contact.

The AWACS did. The airborne controller identified the two Iraqi planes rising off the runway as MiG-29s and said they were on course for a flight of F-111s and a lone A-10, which was orbiting in the bushes at ten o'clock.

"Drop tanks," Hack ordered his wingmate. Letting go of

the extra fuel rigs beneath their wings would increase the F-15s' maneuverability and speed.

Didn't help the radar, though. He couldn't even find the A-10.

Saw the F-111s, cutting hard to the west, out of the line of fire.

The radio blared with static and more cross talk. The AWACS controller asked for silence on the circuit, his voice several octaves higher than at the start of the mission. Then he gave Hack and Johnny a new vector.

"Okay, okay," Hack shouted as the Eagle's APG-63 radar flicked two contacts about where the MiGs should be, ghosting them on the heads-up display at the front of the glass. That didn't absolutely mean it had found the Iraqis— the vast majority of planes in the air were Coalition bombers tearing up Iraq, and they couldn't all be counted on to be where they were supposed to be. And he still hadn't found the A-10, which he assumed would have a wingmate somewhere behind him. Hack "tickled" the contacts with the Eagle's electronic query system, checking the planes for their IDs.

No IDs.

MiGs. Or coalition planes too shot up to have working transponders.

Possible. Where was that damn A-10?

"I'm spiked!" Johnny yelled. An unfriendly radar had found and targeted him—and they hadn't even sorted the enemy fighters yet. "That MiG is on me."

One of the unidentified contacts disappeared from Hack's radar. He didn't have time to wonder why—the other, apparently the one that had turned its radar onto Johnny, began angling for his wingmate.

Bandit?

Or a confused allied plane with battle damage?

The Eagles and the unidentified contact were moving toward each other now at just under 1,200 miles an hour. They were thirty miles apart; Hack had sixty seconds to decide whether to fire.

Maybe less. The RWR warned that a ground radar ahead had begun tracking him. Hack ignored it, trusting that the Eagle's ECMs and his altitude would protect him, at least for the moment.

The bottom of Hack's heads-up display indicated he had four Sparrow III AIM-7 air-to-air missiles, ready to go. He took a breath, narrowing his focus on the boogie. He was just coming into range.

He queried again. Still no ID. His heart was pounding on overdrive, but something in his head was warning him away—the plane wasn't acting like a MiG, he thought.

"Tiger, I'm locked on a target," he told the AWACS controller as calmly as possible. "I want IDs. I can't find that A-10."

But the transmission was overrun. He tried again; if he got through he didn't hear the reply.

"Piranha One, I'm still spiked," said Johnny.

If the boogie was a MiG-29 with beyond-visual-range weapons, Hack's wingmate was going to be history in about twenty seconds.

If it was a beat-up Warthog, friendly fire was going to claim its first victim of the air war.

"Fox One, Fox One!" he shouted to his wingmate, warning him that he was firing a medium-range radar missile.

19

As soon as Doberman heard the Eagle pilot call the radar missile shot, he slammed his plane back toward Wong and the rest of the Snake Eaters ground team. Their radio frequency fuzzed with static; he worried that maybe the MiGs had been coming after them.

"Devil One, this is Snake Eater. Please reply," said Wong finally. The transmission crackled and broke up.

"Devil One," said Doberman, pointing his nose back in the direction of the highway. He was roughly eight miles south of the village. "Wong, you got a target for me?" he snapped.

"We have a tel erector approximately three miles west of Kajuk beneath a culvert on the highway," Wong told him.

"Okay, good. Yeah, okay." Doberman could see the hill in front of him on the left; the culvert would be almost dead-on. He immediately began a sharp turn west, deciding to work the Hog down to a thousand feet for the attack. He'd swoop out of the north, turning around the village, riding down toward the culvert, trade a little bit of angle for a longer, better view.

"There are other developments," said Wong before he had completed his turn.

"Yeah?"

"A Gaskin SA-9 mobile launcher has been set up on the hill behind the erector, immediately to the north. Excuse me," added Wong. "I'm told another is approaching."

Doberman cursed. The Gaskin was a seventies-era missile with a heat-seeking warhead. Compared with missiles like the SA-2, its range and altitude were relatively limited—but it was sitting just to the side of his attack route.

It would fire as soon as he pulled off. He could goose off diversionary flares and jerk his butt around, but it'd be tight.

At best.

Doberman's eyes hunted through the terrain, spotting the hills where the village was located. He was too far away to make out any buildings there, let alone the highway and SAMs.

He could go for the antiair first, but that would be a bitch with two of them. By the time he splashed the first—if he splashed the first—the second might be ready to fire.

"Give me the layout, Wong," he said. "Are those SAMs set up or what?"

"One definitely is. The other is taking position at the south side of the road. The mean time for launch—"

"Yeah, yeah, okay."

It was too risky. Especially since he'd have a hard time seeing the launcher under the roadway.

Worth it if he could be sure he was getting missiles—especially if they had chemical warheads.

Hell, if he had to bail he could always hook up with Wong and his Delta Force buddies. Wouldn't that be fun?

"What about the Scuds themselves?" he asked Wong. "Are they there?"

"We're working on it, Captain. Please be patient."

"I have less than twelve minutes of fuel to play with," Doberman said. "Don't take all day."

He banked the Hog westward, barely missing the SAMs' theoretical targeting envelope. They could hit a tailpipe from five miles out.

Best thing to do, get low and go after the SA-9s first. Fifty feet head-on, no way they'd nail him.

Could be get both launchers in one run?

The Iraqis would have to be pretty stupid to line them up for him.

Duh.

"Devil One, we have a pickup truck entering the village. We are observing it now. It appears to be a command vehicle," added Wong. "Please stand by."

Doberman jostled his legs and arms nervously. He felt like he was waiting on the express line at a supermarket with a week's thirst and a six-pack in his hand, stuck behind a fat lady with a month's supply of groceries.

The woman morphed into Rosen.

This was not the time to be distracted. Doberman pushed his head down and ran through the instrument readings, trying for a routine, trying to keep his edge and his focus. He began a steady climb as he slid his orbit farther north toward the river. He turned and lined up to come into Al-Kajuk with the Avenger cannon blazing. All he needed was a target. He'd smoke it, then use the hill for cover from the SAMs.

Tight, but doable.

"Come on, Wong, what's the story?" said Doberman. "Is that pickup truck heading anywhere, or what?"

"We've found the storage facility," said Wong finally. "We believe we have identified two missiles, but we do not have a positive confirmation."

"That's enough for me. I'm going in," he said, bolting upright against his seat restraints. "Give me directions. I have that tower thing dead-on."

"The tower thing," Wong said, "is a minaret, and it is part of the target. We believe the missiles are being stored in a mosque."

"Repeat?"

"Affirmative, a mosque. Please break off your attack until we have received authorization for the strike."

"Son of a shit," said Doberman. Standing orders prevented an attack on a mosque.

"Repeat?"

Mosque or no mosque, if there were Scuds with chemical warheads down there, they needed to be taken out. He could see the building in the lower right quadrant of his screen.

In five seconds he'd cross into the SA-9s' range. They were going to get a strong whiff of his exhaust if he waited any longer to turn.

"Captain Glenon?"

"Yeah, I'm breaking off," he told Wong. "Let's think this through. I'm going to be bingo pretty damn quick and have to go back to Al-Jouf. Shit."

20

By the time the two F-15s had recovered from their evasive maneuvers, the MiG had disappeared from the screen. Hack knew that his missile had missed; he blamed himself for waiting too long, probably giving the Iraqi time to hit his countermeasures and run away.

He and his wingmate swept north, their radars once again beating the weeds.

Hack's screen popped up a fresh contact at a bare thousand feet, almost dead ahead.

Exactly where the MiG would be if it had hit its afterburners and dove into the ground effects, trying to duck his radar.

"I have a contact," he told Johnny, giving him a bearing. "We're close, we're close."

"You got a visual?"

"Negative. I'm locked," Hack told him.

"I'm tickling—shit, shit, he's friendly, he's ours, he's ours! Don't fire! Don't fire!"

Hack cursed, too—the plane his radar had just locked up was an A-10A Warthog.

What the hell was it doing way up here? It sure as hell wasn't on the Air Tasking Order, at least not that he had seen.

The AWACS controller was yelping in his ear.

"Piranha One acknowledges," Hack said coolly. "I understand that is a friendly. Tell him not to sweat it. We're coming south."

"Probably doesn't even know you had him by the short hairs," said Johnny as they turned to head south for Saudi territory and their waiting KC-135.

Hack didn't answer. He suddenly felt angry as hell at the Warthog and its driver, as if the plane had made him miss the MiG.

Damn Warthogs had no business being in the war, let alone being so deep in Iraq. They were old, obsolete, slow, and worst of all, ugly.

Hack ought to know: he'd been a Hog driver for nearly three years before finally kissing enough ass to get promoted to the real Air Force.

Damn stinking Warthog and its dumb-as-shit drivers. Probably got lost.

He checked his position and heading, then flicked the radar into air-to-air scan, hunting for his tanker.

21

Even a Hog driver had his limits.

After nearly twenty minutes of temptation and a ho-hum flight back toward Al-Jouf, Shotgun was overcome by boredom as much as hunger. He reached down to the pocket flap for the Twinkie. The cellophane wrapper teased his fingertips—he rarely wore flight gloves—but the package had somehow wedged itself in the bottom of his pocket and resisted his gentle tug. Under ordinary circumstances, Shotgun would just yank, squeeze, and swallow, but with your last piece of pastry you had to consider karma. Squishing the delicate icing was very bad luck, especially while you were still over enemy territory. So he leaned down, trying to slip his fingers beneath the cardboard at the base of the pastry and tease it out.

As he did, his eyes caught something on the ground

ahead, a small gray shape scuttling along like a crab in a
shallow pool. Shotgun left the Twinkie in his pocket and
jerked upright in the seat. A Zil truck with a trailer was running across the desert ahead, maybe ten miles from the
Saudi border. This wasn't some Iraqi dad taking his kid to
college—the trailer was a 122mm D-30 towed howitzer, a
large and effective medium-range artillery piece designed
to harass well-meaning trespassers and Coalition troops on
the good-guy side of the border.

The Hog sniffed and snorted, her appetite inflamed by
the tasty treat. She was in almost perfect position to gobble
it up; a good solid push on the stick, perhaps a tad of rudder, and the target would slide into the cannon's crosshairs
at maybe five thousand feet. Shotgun pushed in, so excited
by his good fortune that he forgot he was flying with only
one engine.

The A-10A promptly reminded him, bucking her tail behind him. It didn't amount to more than a slight whimper of
complaint, however—Shotgun barely noticed as the altitude ladder on his HUD scrolled downward, falling
promptly through eight thousand to seven thousand feet. At
six thousand, the truck passed into his targeting pipper, but
Shotgun held off, deciding that he would bank behind the
truck and come lower, attacking it from the rear with a long,
shallow approach, a tactical concession to the fact that he
was running with only one engine.

Technically, of course, the concession he should have
made was to ignore the target and fly directly back to base.
But Shotgun had never considered himself a technical type.
He banked and came around, down now to nearly three
thousand feet, a turkey shoot except that the Zil was not
only moving faster than he thought but had cut to his right,

leaving whatever trail it was following to dart and dodge in the hard-packed sand. Shotgun corrected but then threw his momentum too far to the right, not only completely losing the shot but nearly putting himself into a spin.

Never again would he fly without a reserve supply of Twizzlers. Never.

He sighed, straightening the plane and circling back in a long arc, the target now running toward him in the left corner of his windscreen. Shotgun kissed the stick with his fingertips, pulling the Hog's nose onto the radiator of the Zil as he nailed the trigger home. The gun roared as he gave the Gat a good double pump, a personal-signature kind of thing. The cannon's recoil practically stopped him in midair, the plane jittering as her nose erupted with flames and smoke from the gun.

As he let off on the trigger, Shotgun realized two things: (1) he'd blown the shot, because the truck was still moving; (2) things were suddenly awful quiet.

The shock of the recoil had flamed the plane's one good engine. Under other circumstances, Shotgun would have undone his seat restraints and given himself a good kick in the rumpus area for flying like such an idiot. But he was down to two thousand feet, not a particularly good place to fly without means of propulsion. And besides, he was already being chewed out sufficiently by the plane's warning lights. He nosed down for momentum, cursing over the stall warning as he worked to restart. The turbines spun, the fuel combusted, and the GE turbofan on the left side of the hull kicked herself back to life. The Hog lurched and he managed to pull out maybe three seconds before his job description would have changed from pilot to backhoe operator.

Any other pilot would have called it a day and set sail for the Saudi border a few miles away. But whatever other characteristics he possessed, Shotgun was not a quitter. He had a very deep sense of obligation, and realized that his boneheaded stupidity had just brought serious embarrassment to Hog drivers everywhere. True, he had an excuse—obviously his blood sugar was out of whack. But how could he take his place in the great fraternity of Hog men, to say nothing of tomorrow night's poker game, knowing that he had missed an easy shot on an unprotected target?

He couldn't just go in with the cannon now. It wasn't simply that he might flame the engine again. Hardly. That could be avoided or at least prepared for by simply climbing higher and attacking with a steeper angle. But doing that would be tantamount to admitting he was unworthy; it would be expected, it would be boring. The stakes had been raised. Shotgun had to go beyond the mundane. Hog drivers the world over were counting on him to demonstrate élan and ingenuity.

There was, fortunately, a way.

Shotgun steadied the Hog at roughly twelve hundred feet over the desert, banking two miles behind the Zil. Nudging his nose into the swirling grit, he picked up speed as he hurtled toward the rear of the truck. The Hog coughed for a second, wondering what he was up to, but Shotgun kept on, his timing and aim perfect. He caught up to the Zil and whipped his right wing up in a terrific banking turn maybe three feet in front of the windshield, swooping into the driver's vision so suddenly that the man yanked the wheel hard to the left, toppling the truck and trashing the howitzer behind him.

Shotgun's wingtip was two feet off the road before he

slapped the plane back level. He belatedly realized he could have smashed the truck's windshield if he'd popped his landing gear at the right moment.

But that was Monday-morning quarterbacking. The truck and its trailer lay sprawled upside down in the desert sand, the howitzer broken in a half.

Shotgun checked his course for Al-Jouf, did a quick instrument check, and then reached down for the Twinkie.

Which, shaken loose by the encounter with the Zil, slid right into his fingers, demanding to be eaten.

22

Captain Wong cast an eye toward the dark speck in the sky to the west as he continued to talk to its pilot over the satellite communications system. The Hog was undoubtedly into its fuel reserves and ought to head back to Al-Jouf. But Captain Glenon was as stubborn as the dogs he'd been nicknamed for.

"There is no need for us to call a strike in on the mosque," Wong told Doberman, speaking slowly into the Satcom's retro-black-plastic and steel handset. The radio consisted of the control unit rucksack and an antenna "dish" that looked like a large X fashioned from thin, flat metal blades. "If the Iraqis follow their usual pattern, they will move the missiles as dusk falls, perhaps slightly afterward. It will then be rather easy to attack them. I would expect an approximate time of 1900 hours."

"Yeah, all right," said Doberman. "I'll be back."

Wong shook his head. It wasn't that he didn't think Doberman could get back in time; on the contrary, given the legendary efficiency of the A-10A maintenance crews, not to mention Captain Glenon's own snappy manner, he could undoubtedly rearm and return with four or five minutes to spare. The Hog, however, was not a night fighter; if the Iraqis deviated from their normal pattern, or simply ran late, he would have a difficult time locating his target. He was also flying without a wingman—a dubious situation at best.

Wong would have to request fresh air support. But it was useless to tell this to Doberman, who would only complain and curse. Captain Glenon was even more cantankerous and aggressive than the average Hog driver. Wong had a theory that this was due in large measure to his small stature—so little place to store the bad humors the body naturally accumulated.

He didn't bother sharing the theory with Doberman. Nor did he tell him it was unnecessary to return—he could let the AWACS operator relay the message after a new strike team was designated.

"Roger your transmission," Wong said simply. "Thanks for your help."

"Yeah, right," said Doberman.

Wong clicked off the circuit and turned back toward the communications specialist, intending to ask him to contact the AWACS while he went and checked on the rest of the team.

The com specialist had his hands spread out wide. A few yards down the hill, six Iraqis were pointing guns at them. One of the soldiers gestured toward Wong, indicating that the captain should raise his hands and step away from the radio.

It seemed expedient to comply, and so he did.

PART TWO

LOST AIRMAN

1

Air Force Technical Sergeant Rebecca "Becky" Rosen plopped her tired body down against a Spec Ops rucksack and leaned against the inside wall of the shelter. For the first time since parachuting into Fort Apache, she had nothing to do—no Hog to fix, no Army helicopter to rebuild. Fatigue surged over her like the green-blue waves of the Atlantic, salty and cold, numbing her feet and stinging her nostrils. But as tired as she was, Rosen couldn't allow herself to fall asleep. The unit was evacuating south as soon as night fell; she was afraid if she dozed off now she'd never manage to wake herself when needed. So she reached beneath her jacket and pulled out the small spiral-bound notebook she'd carried with her since coming to Iraq some weeks back. Rosen had been intending to keep a journal of the deployment but until now had only made three one-word notes, each for a different day, and each confined to the weather— rain, cold, clear, in that order. Folding the book open to a blank page, she retrieved the silver-plated Cross pen from her breast pocket, sliding her calloused fingertips across the smooth metal. The pen had been a present from a college professor, and she thought of him now, thought of his classes in Shakespeare and his funny pronunciations of words, a mix of British and down-home Texas accents.

Shoehorning her studies around her duties as an Air Force NCO, Rosen had managed a degree in English literature. She didn't care about the degree; she wasn't going to do anything with it. But that was the point. Poetry tickled a side of her she hadn't realized existed until a friend talked her into signing up for a continuing-ed class so it wouldn't be canceled for lack of students. Becky Rosen was a mechanic. She saw things with her hands, whether they were Hog avionics systems or busted AH-6 engines. She'd been fixing things since she helped her uncle rebuild a Ford high-compression 302 when she was seven. The real world was physical, in your face; Becky Rosen had overcome a for-shit childhood and done well, but she'd also had her fingers mashed, and a hell of a lot of worse, along the way. Literature, poetry especially, seemed like an exotic vacation of dreams, relief from the real world's fumes and acid. Shakespeare, Wordsworth, Donne, Pound, Whitman, Eliot—they were lands far away she could disappear to. The harsh rhythms of Gerard Manley Hopkins, the delicate balance of Byron, the false bravado of Dylan Thomas—all offered shelter.

Dylan Thomas had told his father on his deathbed to fight to the end, to scream against his fate.

Had Lieutenant Dixon screamed in that final moment before he'd been shot?

She saw Dixon now in the dirt on the hill next to Sugar Mountain, facedown, body limp, limbs askew. He'd been such a nice kid, quiet but brave. Or foolish, maybe—he'd volunteered as a forward ground controller, working with Delta Force behind the lines.

No more foolish than she'd been, volunteering for this mission. In her mind at the time, there was no choice—she had been the only person at Al-Jouf capable of getting the Special Operations helos back together. But a lot of people might think it foolish.

Definitely. To say nothing of being against regulations and probably the law.

Not the time or place to worry about it. Rosen twisted the pen carefully so the point extended. She began to write:

Jan. 25.
Iraq. How I got here is a long story. It started

She held the pen up from the paper. There was always a possibility of being captured. She had to watch what she wrote.

Rosen scratched out the words and began again:

Jan. 25.
Iraq. How I got here is a long story, to be told later.
All I can say is it was a hell of a trip.
I saw a dead man today, my first, believe it or not.
I loved him.

Tears erupted from her eyes and she began to shake uncontrollably.

She loved him?

Yes. She'd never admitted it until now, let alone told him or anyone else. But they'd kissed once, a moment stolen in the dark back at King Fahd.

They'd kissed.

The only time in the Air Force that she'd really, truly felt something like that, felt the steel hooks in her gut, felt love.

One kiss, all she had.

2

Dixon knew it was a Hog the instant he heard the sound, even though the plane was so far away the sound was less than a whisper. He froze, eyes upward, exposed near the highway he'd been following. The sound faded completely, a tease or a delusion.

Except he knew it wasn't. He saw a dot passing in the sky overhead, far overhead.

A Hog. One of his squadron mates. Had to be.

And then it was gone. He stared upward for a long time, more than a half hour, until he heard another sound, this one much closer. He turned his head and realized it was a truck, driving toward him.

Dazed as he was by hunger and fatigue, it took forever to get his legs in motion. Dixon took a step in exactly the wrong direction, toward the highway; in agonizingly slow motion he twisted his body back, clutching the rifle to his belly. He spotted a clump of low trees ahead. The ground sloped upward behind it into a large, squat hill, half-covered with vegetation. Another hill, this one much lower and nearly all rock and dirt, lay to the left. He could see the roof of a building beyond the trees as he ran, and realized the dirt included a dusty, primitive roadway.

His side hurt, but there was no choice but to keep running. He could hear the truck on the highway behind him slowing to a stop. He threw himself down as it whined into reverse.

Had they seen him? Dixon twisted around to look. The truck was coming in his direction over the dirt road, but it was still a good way off.

He had to assume they had seen him. In any event, if he stayed here very much longer they surely would. Perhaps with the shadows he might make the low trees without being seen.

Dixon pushed himself back to his feet, stooping forward as he ran. He made the trees; the truck was on the road, moving slowly, but still coming. A small house made of painted clay or cement lay on his right, ringed by upright stubs that could be parts of old trees or perhaps abandoned fence posts. The doorway was open; it looked empty. Dixon considered running for it but changed his mind. If they'd seen him, it would be the first place they'd look.

The dirt road veered between the large hill on the right and the smaller one on the left. Fifty yards ahead, up a bald slope on the left, an old car sat near a dilapidated stone wall. Dixon pushed his rifle butt into the stitch in his side and ran for it. The ground flew behind him, pain and confusion narrowing his vision as he dove headfirst over the rocks, rolling in the dust, out of breath. His chest and throat heaved; he fought against the reflex and swung around, checking the AK-47's clip as he leaned low against the rocks.

The truck, a pickup, steered gingerly along the road, dodging rocks. It was not only new but seemingly immaculate, the white body gleaming as if freshly waxed. It stopped in front of the house.

Dixon saw that there were only two men inside—he might have a chance if they came for him.

They didn't. The truck lurched forward, resuming its slow crawl around the rocks in the road. It began picking up speed as it followed the path around the base of the hill to the left.

Dixon waited until he could breathe normally again. Then he eyed the house carefully. He saw something move around the back, then realized there were animals there, two dogs and a goat. The dogs seemed to be tied to one of the stubby trees; the goat grazed on slivers of vegetation.

Food.

Someone would be inside the house.

The ground went up sharply behind the building, climbing through brush. There didn't seem to be an easy way to circle around; he'd have to expose himself by walking along the road where the pickup truck had gone.

Better off going for it. Come straight in the front door, Hog style, gun ready.

He'd kill whoever was in there. No one was a civilian as far as he was concerned. No one. That was the way he had to think—had to act—if he was going to survive long enough to blow up the missiles he'd seen. Otherwise, he might just as well shoot himself now and be done with it.

He'd never do that.

Dixon slid to his knees, stretching his arms out before him. A few low bushes and some sort of farm tool—it seemed to be a dilapidated plow—lay between the road and the house. Neither they nor the narrow stubs of sticks would offer real cover.

If he were back home in Wisconsin, there'd be a farmer, a wife, a kid or two inside. Cat to match the dogs, maybe two. They'd be preoccupied, getting dinner.

Dixon pushed himself to his feet, rifle propped in the crook of his elbow. He had the gun and his wits and his hunger. He moved slowly at first, then realized it was better to go quickly; he began to trot forward. If the open field gave him no cover, it meant none for his enemies either. He pointed the AK-47 at the doorway, eyes scanning back and forth across the front of the building, aware he could be attacked from the corners or the lone window.

Twenty yards from the house, he stopped. The dogs began to bark, but he could tell they weren't barking at him. They'd run behind the house, had seen or smelled something more interesting.

Dixon crouched, waiting for something to happen. The small house had no telephone wires, no power lines, no antenna that he could see. No house in America would be this small. Its walls were the color of the dirt—light brown with tinges of dark brown, streaks of blood that had dried.

Something moved behind the window. Dixon raised his rifle, waited.

Nothing.

A shadow, or his imagination.

He got out of the crouch, began walking forward, gun

moving slowly back and forth across the face of the building, ready.

Nothing.

The dogs had stopped barking around the back.

A figure appeared in the doorway.

It was a woman in a long, dirty white dress. She looked across the yard directly into his eyes, locking him with her stare.

Part of him truly meant to shoot her. Part of him truly realized that he had no friends here, that he could not afford to think of anyone as a civilian.

A larger part could not find the will to squeeze the trigger. He stood stock-still, gun lowered to the ground.

The woman raised her right hand. His first thought was that she had a gun. Then he saw she was simply gesturing, raising both arms as if to plead with him.

For help? To come? To go?

In the next instant, Dixon dove to the ground, ducking as gunfire erupted from behind and inside the building.

3

As varied and multifaceted as his career in the armed forces
had been, Bristol Wong had never once been captured. He
hadn't even studied the phenomenon thoroughly; while he
could cite to within a centimeter the target envelope of any
Soviet-made missile from Scud to SS-25 ICBM, he had only
the dimmest notion of the Geneva Conventions governing
prisoners. The various survival courses he had taken, including both Navy and Air Force SERE School, provided
relatively skimpy background; it was difficult to duplicate
the experience of cold metal being pressed against the side
of your neck nearly two hundred miles inside enemy territory.

Actually, the metal, which belonged to the business end
of an AK-47, seemed a little warm. The man holding the gun
had just finished searching him, efficiently removing his

ammunition as well as his personal weapons. He now jerked the barrel of his assault rifle against Wong's neck, motioning that Wong should kneel on the ground next to the Satcom.

Wong glanced at the Iraqi commander, a squat man in light brown khakis holding a pistol a few feet away. Then he slowly lowered himself to the ground, unsure what the Iraqis intended. The Delta Force com specialist stood two yards away to Wong's right, three Iraqi AK-47s in his chest. Even if he'd been wearing body armor, any twitch would end the sergeant's life.

The Iraqi commander told him in Arabic to contact his base and say there was no problem. Wong pretended not to understand.

"What exactly do you wish done?" Wong said in English.

"Tell whomever you were communicating with that there is no problem," said the man in flawless English.

Wong nodded and bent to the com unit, but before he could touch the Satcom's controls, a bullet zipped into the dirt about a foot away. He froze, calling on an old Yoga breathing exercise to empty his lungs slowly.

"There is an emergency beacon on your radio, I assume," said the captain.

"I'm unaware of any," said Wong.

"Back away from it," said the man.

Wong straightened and took a step back. The Iraqi's game intrigued him; he'd obviously had no intention of allowing Wong to use the device but wanted to study his reactions.

"I will shoot you if I wish," said the Iraqi captain.

"Naturally."

"Your job is to make me not wish to do that," said the Iraqi. "Why are you here?"

"I am a spy," said Wong.

The captain began to laugh. He told his men in Arabic what Wong had said. An honest spy, he called him. Then he turned back to Wong.

"We shoot spies at dawn," the captain said.

"I would expect so."

"What were you spying on?"

"Your defenses," said Wong.

"And what did you find here?"

"They appear formidable."

The captain raised the barrel of his AK-47 so that it was aimed at Wong's head. Technically speaking, that was not as intimidating as it would have been had it been pointing toward his chest; he held the gun with only one hand, unbraced, and Wong realized that even at this range it was likely to jerk off target. Still, it delivered the appropriate message.

"What are you really looking for, Captain?" asked the Iraqi. "Who are you looking for?"

Who—significant, undoubtedly.

"If I came here knowing what I would find, there would have been little sense in coming," said Wong.

"How did you get here?"

"I walked."

The Iraqi captain jerked the gun away and fired into the dirt in front of his feet. The ground was soft enough for the bullets to penetrate and there were no ricochets, but Wong saw that the men who were holding their weapons on the sergeant jumped with the sound. All had their fingers on the triggers of their weapons; the odds against an accidental firing were not particularly good.

"I ask you again, how did you get here?"

"As I said, I hiked here. I would have liked to have run, but as you can tell, I am not in particularly top condition; it was more like a walk."

"You walked from Saudi Arabia?"

"Of course not."

The Iraqi smiled again. Wong thought he could place the accent in the man's English around Chicago. He guessed the Iraqi had gone to college or university in Illinois.

"And what did you do before you walked?"

"I parachuted."

"You're a parachutist?" The man laughed, as if genuinely questioning Wong's qualifications.

"I hold a USPA Class-D skydiving license, with gold wings, ruby badges, and instructor certification," said Wong. "If you wish I can recite my entire jump résumé, beginning with my first free fall on a tethered jump at age ten—an illegal dive, incidentally, from which, fortunately, there were no repercussions."

"What the hell are you, Captain?" asked the Iraqi.

"I am a spy," said Wong. "Captain Bristol Wong, U.S. Air Force."

The Iraqi shook his head, then turned to the sergeant. "And you—are you a spy as well?"

The sergeant recited his name, rank, and serial number. The Iraqi moved his head slightly; one of the men guarding the com specialist crashed his rifle butt into his side, sending him to the ground.

"There is no need for that," said Wong. "I will cooperate with you. The sergeant is merely an enlisted man of no importance."

"And the rest of your men?"

Wong had considered how to answer the question and

decided that a lie was most expedient, even if it wasn't believed. It would at least give the rest of the team a chance to escape.

"There are no other men," he said.

"American spies do not travel alone," said the captain. "Especially when they are part of Delta Force."

An interesting gambit, Wong thought. The patrol's uniforms were unmarked, and in theory there was no way to know that they were Delta or Green Berets. But of course Delta was famous, and it was no secret that they were in the Gulf. Any Iraqi would guess that clandestine operations would be carried out by them. And it would certainly bring cachet to claim to have captured some.

"I myself am Air Force," said Wong. "My sergeant is a soldier. We do have ambitions, however."

"Ambitions?"

"It is an honor to join Delta Force," said Wong, watching to see how the man reacted. "And perhaps someday, after we prove our worthiness, we will achieve that stature."

"That day will be in another life," said the Iraqi commander.

One of his men shouted from the other side of the ridge, calling his commander and urging him to come and inspect something they had found. The Iraqi told one of the soldiers guarding the sergeant to come with him; the others were to make sure the sergeant and Wong didn't move.

"And watch this one," added the captain, pointing his gun at Wong before going. "He speaks Arabic, though he pretends not to. Very clever for a spy."

4

Doberman cursed as he heard the controller at Al-Jouf give priority to a battle-stricken Tornado, freezing the landing queue so the British jet could make an emergency landing. While the long stretch of Saudi concrete had been envisioned as a forward operating area for Hogs and Spec Ops troops, the base had quickly become a life raft for battle-damaged Coalition planes. It made for a busy pattern. Besides the Tornado—a two-seat recon type that could use ground-following radar for a quick and hard run over enemy territory—a French Jaguar and an Australian C-130 were slotted between another Hog and an F-16 ahead of Doberman in the aerial traffic jam.

Even less patient than normal, Doberman considered declaring a fuel emergency to get himself pushed to the head of the line. He had plenty of fuel, however, even though he'd goosed the Hog well over four hundred knots all the way back. And he had to give the crew of Special Operations air controllers and support personnel handling Al-Jouf their due—they were clearing planes in quicker than O'Hare on Christmas Eve.

Once upon a time, landing had been fraught with anxiety for him. But now it was routine, or as close to routine as he'd allow anything to become, afraid that if he got too used to it he'd take it for granted. He settled into his seat as he rounded onto the last leg of the approach pattern. The Hog's indicated airspeed plummeted toward double digits. Gear out, air brakes deployed, he looked the long splash of concrete into his windshield. Doberman pushed his chest forward and head up as the wheels made a whumping sound, nudging against the pavement; he peered out of the cockpit like a kid watching a baseball game over a picket fence. A fuel truck headed a line six planes deep at the far end of the access ramp; he cursed when he saw that, convinced that he'd be stuck here until nightfall. He turned off the runway onto the ramp, treading past a parked MC-130, a black-painted Hercules used for Special Ops missions, then spotted another Hog off to his right; the dark "DS" on the tail told him it was Shotgun's. He couldn't see his wingman, but two Delta troopers were standing at full attention near it. That gave him an idea—he pulled on his rudders and wheeled next to the plane, spinning around so his nose was pointed for a quick getaway. He powered down and popped the canopy, whipping off his helmet and restraints.

"Yo, you guys work for Klee, right?" he yelled down to the troopers. Klee was the Delta Force colonel in charge of most of the American Special Operations troops at Al-Jouf as well as those working with Apache.

The soldiers couldn't hear him with all the noise at the base. Doberman was in such a hurry he didn't bother cranking down the cockpit ladder—he rolled himself right off the side of the plane, his hands gripping and then slipping off the fairing at the side of the cockpit. He landed on his feet, but just barely, the shock of the concrete reverberating through his legs.

Not that he was about to let that stop him.

"Yo!" he yelled again, running to the troopers. "You guys work for Colonel Klee, yes?"

One of the Delta operators began to nod.

"I'm Doberman. I need fuel," he told them. "There's a Delta patrol in deep shit up north. I don't care what you do, you get me some jet fuel. Go. Before your friends get fried."

Doberman's last words were unnecessary—the troopers had bolted away. He ran to the port "kneecap"—the housing for the wheel on the left side of the plane. He popped the cover on the refueling controls and gave the gear a quick inspection. Before the war, he'd taken part in two or three exercises where ground soldiers refueled his Hog; in theory everyone on the base could handle it, though he was more than willing to do it himself if it came to that. In the meantime, he needed some candy—bombs, preferably Mavericks. He had just turned to scan the area for ordies, when a bull rammed him from behind.

Not a bull, just Shotgun, pounding him on the back.

"About time you got your butt back here," said Shotgun. He was stuffing a wedge of what seemed to be a birthday cake into his mouth.

Doberman knew better than to ask for details. "I need some candymen," he told Shotgun.

"On their way," Shotgun said. "Two Maverick Gs good enough?"

"Just two?" Doberman asked.

"All I could steal," said Shotgun. He wiped his mouth with his sleeve while reaching into a pocket with his other hand. He pulled out a pair of Hostess cupcakes, wrapped in plastic and somehow not crushed. "You want one?"

"I want some CBUs," said Doberman.

"Cluster bombs are on their way," Shotgun assured him. "Now don't get picky. All we have are standard-issue Mark 20 Rockeyes. I know there's some CBU-71 frag/incendiaries somewhere out here, but they're harder to find than Dunky Donuts coffee. Which is still pretty fresh, by the way, if you're interested."

"No thanks," said Doberman, spotting a quartet of bomb loaders pushing a pair of bomb-laden trucks in his direction.

"Sure you don't want one of these cupcakes?" Shotgun asked. "Got the yellow-goo frosting. Oversized models some Delta chef special ordered. It's what I'm talking about. Serious treats."

"I'll pass," said Doberman, trotting to the candymen. The ordnance specialists were part of the enlisted backbone of the Air Force, generally unrecognized professionals who picked up their lunch pails every morning—or night—and went out to do their job with the practiced precision of a championship football team. The men nodded to the pilot and started positioning their deadly payload on the Hog's hardpoints. The weapons were safed; still, a mistake, even a moment's inattention, could very possibly destroy half the base. Despite this, the crew moved faster than hotel workers positioning boardwalk chairs on a pleasant summer's day. Doberman took a deep breath, his anxiety diminishing. His stomach growled and he realized he might actually be hungry—not surprising since he hadn't eaten anything since taking off from Fort Apache.

"Hey, Gun, maybe I *will* have a cupcake," he told his wingmate.

"Sorry, Dog Man. All gone. How about a Devil Dog? Kinda poetic justice, don't you think?"

The dark brown cake was scrunched, but Doberman took it anyway, swallowing it so quickly that even Shotgun was impressed.

"Maybe you want to go find something to eat in one of the mess areas," Shotgun said. "One of the units has a pig roast going."

"No time," said Doberman, dodging out of the way as a fuel truck barreled up. The two troopers who'd been guarding Shotgun's Hog were on the hood; the truck looked suspiciously like the one that had been at the head of the refueling cue before, but he wasn't about to ask any questions. A staff sergeant jumped from the rear before the truck came to a halt and ran forward with the refueling hose, fireman style. The men were familiar with the procedure and had the nozzle connected before Doberman could say anything. He watched them start the pump and then went back to Shotgun.

"So how's your Hog?" Doberman asked, glancing toward the nearby plane. A pair of ladders stood against the plane's right engine and wing. A gaunt figure loomed from the other side, appearing over the motor as if he had suddenly levitated there.

Tinman, Devil Squadron's ancient mechanic. Doberman half believed he *had* levitated there—the geezer was into some weird Louisiana voodoo witchcraft stuff. With Rosen north, Tinman was responsible for the two Hogs.

"Be up in the air in ten minutes," Shotgun said.

"Knock tenk," shouted Tinman, shaking his head. The technical expert spoke in an indecipherable tongue rumored to be a cross between pidgin English and a deep Bayou dialect.

"Hey, come on, Tinman, it's only an oil leak," Shotgun yelled back. "You can fix that with your eyes closed."

"Isk knock jester oil," said the mechanic, going back to work. The GE's gizzards were exposed; from where Doberman was standing, they looked like a mess.

"Ain't no thing," Shotgun told Doberman. "He just likes to complain. Old guys are like that. Hell, I can fix that motor," he added. "Easier than tuning a Harley. That's what I'm talking about. So what's the story? You bounce the Scuds or what?"

Doberman gave him the executive summary.

"They're going to hold their position and watch for the missiles," he said, glancing at the sun sliding toward the horizon. "I ought to make it back right around the time they're moving them."

"You flying up there solo, Dog Man?"

"You got a better idea?"

"I'm talking ten minutes," said Shotgun.

Tinman slammed a piece of metal on the Hog.

"I can't wait."

"Wong'll probably have somebody else splash the Scuds," said Shotgun.

"Maybe," said Doberman. "But somebody's going to have to cover the fire team. They pulled the helos back to Fort Apache."

"Yeah," said Shotgun. "Sending an MH-60 Blackhawk to grab Wong and the gang after the Scuds are hit."

"Why didn't they use the Blackhawk to get the people out from Apache and keep the AH-6s there?"

"If it made a lot of sense, it wouldn't be an Army operation," said Shotgun. "I think it had to do with the fuel."

Doberman nodded. He was thinking of Rosen, so far behind the lines.

"Don't sweat it, Dog Man. Rosen and Braniac will get back okay," said Shogun. "What I was figuring was, we go up, cover Wong, then help Apache bug out. Just, you know, be in the area. They're doing a rendezvous with a Pave Low about thirty or forty miles north of the border. The Little Birds are going to shuttle back and forth. We can watch."

"Yeah," said Doberman. The ground crew had finished loading the bombs on the wings. There were four cluster bombs, one each on stations four, five, seven, and eight, straddling the wheels. The Mavericks were mounted one apiece at hardpoints three and nine, just outboard of the bombs. The Hog's ECM pod sat at the far end of the right wing; on the left was a twin-rail with a pair of Sidewinder air-to-air missiles.

"Look Gun, I got to go," Doberman told Shotgun, trotting toward his plane.

"I got a pizza comin'," yelled his wingmate. "You sure you don't want some for the road? Sausage, 'shrooms, peppers, meatballs, extra cheese, onions, and anchovies."

Doberman glanced back over his shoulder. Shotgun was grinning, but you never knew—he might actually be telling the truth.

"No thanks," yelled Doberman. "Anchovies give me heartburn. Don't want to be burping when it's time to pickle."

"What I'm talking about," said Shotgun.

5

Colonel Knowlington nodded absentmindedly as the young lieutenant finished briefing him on the squadron's supply of Mavericks and bombs. The two men stood near one of the hangars on the outskirts of Oz, Devil Squadron's maintenance area. A gray-green stack of Mark 82 iron bombs, oldies but goodies, sat nearby. The lieutenant's name was Malory but he reminded Skull of an Israeli pilot he'd met during a liaison assignment in the 1960s. A fellow Phantom jock, the Israeli was the same age as this young man but had already shot down five Arab planes, the mark of an ace. Skull had kept in touch with him—and then written to his family when he went down MIA over Egypt in 1972. His body was never found.

There was no good reason for thinking of him—or the bottle of vodka they'd demolished the first night they met.

"Colonel?"

"Go ahead, Lieutenant," said Skull, pretending his attention had been drawn by a battle-damaged Hog rumbling past on its way to its hangars. The Hog's nose art—a toothy shark's grin—declared it was a member of the proud and venerable 23rd Tactical Fighter Wing, descendants of the famous Flying Tigers led by Claire Chennault during World War II.

All of the one-hundred-some Hogs in the combat theater shared King Fahd as their home drome. On paper, Knowlington's 535th made up an entire wing, though it was currently only at squadron strength. The unit had been cobbled together back in the States bare weeks before the air war began and consisted of planes originally designated for the scrap heap. The pilots and crew dogs were a mixed bag of high-time Hog drivers, green newbies, and hangers-on.

"Riyadh may ask for strict rationing," said the lieutenant, poking himself back into his commander's consciousness. The young man was worried the 535th would run out of Mavericks before the ground war began. The AGMs came in several varieties, with either optical or IR guidance, and were a Hog driver's weapon of choice against tanks and most other meaty targets. They didn't miss, and went boom with authority.

"You don't worry about Riyadh," Knowlington told him. "If we start running short, let me know. I'll make sure we have plenty."

"Yes, sir. Thank you, sir," snapped the lieutenant. He was so new his uniform smelled of wrapper.

Knowlington's indulgent grin waned as he spotted his capo di capo approaching. Sergeant Allen Clyston tended to amble rather than walk, except when he was angry about something—which he obviously was now, because he looked like a bull elephant on a charge.

"Anything else, Lieutenant?" Skull asked.

The young man followed his boss's glance toward the capo. "No, sir," he said, quickly retreating.

"You ain't going to believe this shit," said Clyston, drilling his meaty fists into his sides as he halted in front of his commander. The earth shook as he stomped his feet beneath him.

"What shit are we talking about?"

"You know where Rosen is?" demanded Clyston.

"Out at Al-Jouf keeping our Hogs in the air, no?"

Clyston shook his head. The capo's ability to remain calm in the most adverse circumstances was legendary. He had withstood countless Vietnamese shellings during 'Nam and probably as many inspections by Pentagon bigwigs. But his face was red, and though balled into fists, his fingers trembled.

"You okay, Allen?"

"She's in Iraq!" blurted the sergeant.

"Iraq?"

"It's not bad enough we have to lose a pilot in a bullshit ground exercise where he had no f-ing business being. That's a woman, goddamn it! She shouldn't even be over here. Anything happens to her, I'm killing the sons of bitches myself! And then I'm strangling fucking Klee or whoever it was who sent her there. Goddamn it. God f-ing damn it."

"All right, let's find out what the hell is going on here," said Knowlington. Not entirely sure what the hell was going on—it didn't seem possible that Rosen was actually in Iraq—he took the capo by the arm and began walking him toward Hog Heaven. Clyston's body heaved as he walked; Skull worried he might have a heart attack.

It took a while for the gray-haired chief master sergeant to calm down enough to explain what he'd heard. The information had come back channel via a landline from one of Devil Squadron's own maintenance geeks at Al-Jouf. Basically, the team holding down Fort Apache had lost a helo and needed someone to fix it. With no one else available, Rosen had volunteered—and been parachuted in from thirty thousand feet with Captain Bristol Wong, Devil Squadron's intelligence specialist.

"What the hell does Rosen know about helicopters?" Skull asked.

"Nothing," said Clyston. "F-ing nothing."

Knowlington suspected that wasn't entirely true; Technical Sergeant Rosen was, in fact, qualified as an expert in several areas outside of avionics, her primary specialty for Devil Squadron. After Clyston and perhaps one or two of the other top sergeants, she was the best mechanic on the base—huge praise, given the Hog community's tough standards.

But she was a woman, and no way—no, no, no way—should she be in Iraq. Klee or whoever was responsible had gone too far.

Knowlington picked up the phone and called a friend—the general in charge of the operation over at the Special Ops Bat Cave.

"I want an explanation," he started, calm as ice. When the general asked what the hell he was talking about, Knowlington spoke in slow, measured tones, repeating the bare bones of what Clyston had told him.

It was all news to the general.

"We're pulling the Apache team out tonight, Mikey," the general told him. "This is the first I've heard about your people being up there on the ground."

"I expect to see Rosen and Wong standing in front of my desk here at 0600," Skull said calmly.

"You can count on it," answered the general. "Excuse me, I have some heads to chop off."

Clyston's large frame hung over the sides of the small metal chair across from him as Skull put down the phone. The capo had calmed down some and his fingers had stopped shaking, but he looked old. Knowlington wondered if he looked that old himself sometimes.

Probably worse.

"What'd the general say?" asked Clyston.

"They'll be back in the morning."

"That was a two-star you were trashing?"

"I thought I was pretty calm."

Clyston smiled—it was weak, but at least his spirits were moving in the right direction. "Thanks."

Skull nodded. Clyston didn't say anything else or make a move to get up. It was senseless telling Clyston that Rosen would be all right—they'd both been around too long to feed each other feel-good lines. So he changed the subject, telling his first sergeant he was thinking of making Captain Glenon the squadron DO.

"He's got seniority and he's a good pilot," Skull told the squadron's first sergeant. "What do you think?"

The capo nodded. "His temper's the only problem."

"I know," said Knowlington.

"Crew respects him. He's fair. I think he's only hot-headed with people who outrank him."

Knowlington smiled. At the moment he was the only one in the squadron who outranked the short, fiery Hog driver. But he didn't mind aggressive subordinates; on the contrary—he liked someone with an edge to keep him sharp.

"I think he's a good choice," added Clyston. "A lot better than bringing someone in from the outside."

"I don't disagree," said Knowlington. He waited a moment, but Clyston still made no sign of being ready to leave. "We going to be ready for tomorrow's frag?" he asked.

"Oh yeah, all the planes are set. Something was flaky with the landing gear on Devil Seven, but I had Harvey overhaul it. I think Smokes just landed too hard because he had to take a leak."

Clyston grinned, but he still wasn't back to normal. Skull wanted to say something else reassuring, but couldn't think of what that would be. Some commanders had a knack for the right word; he always felt tongue-tied.

"Well, hell, I guess I got some work to get to," said the sergeant.

"Me, too," said Knowlington, rising.

But Clyston lingered a moment longer. He had a question—and Skull suddenly realized it wasn't about Rosen but about him.

Clyston wanted to know if he was drinking again. He'd smelled the Depot on him earlier, maybe saw him coming from that direction. There might even be rumors.

Knowlington wanted to tell him he wasn't. He wanted to admit, too, that he'd been tempted. That he was still tempted, that he'd always be tempted. That maybe he was only a short walk away from plunging back into the numb hole he'd so recently escaped.

Skull opened his mouth, not sure exactly what the words would be. But before any came out, the sergeant nodded and left the office.

6

Captain Hawkins watched as the two AH-6 Little Birds skimmed along the desert terrain toward the landing strip. The two helos were flying maybe three feet from the ground, moving at over a hundred and thirty miles an hour. Tornadoes of dust whipped behind them, as if they were chewing up the dirt and spitting it out.

Hawkins wanted to do something like that, maybe punch and kick it, though he was far too disciplined a soldier to reveal anything approaching the frustration he felt in front of his men. He wanted to ignore the order to withdraw, wanted to grab the phone and call Riyadh or Washington or wherever the damn order originated, yell and scream and tell them how stupid it was to leave now that they were just getting settled.

But he wouldn't. He wasn't even going to share his opinion. He was going to get the two dozen people here, and their equipment, out safely.

"Captain?"

Hawkins turned to Rosen. The diminutive tech sergeant had a bag of tools in her hand that looked to weigh more than she did.

"Yes, Sergeant?"

"I'd like to make sure my fixes are holding," she told him.

"As long as you can do it while they're refueling."

"Yes, sir. How did the strike at Al-Kajuk go? We get the Scuds?"

"Not yet," he told her. "They ran into some targeting problems. I had to order the helos back so we can bug out. Blackhawk's going to pick them up later on."

Rosen nodded.

"You're in the first team out," he added. Because the helicopters were so small—fitting five people in them was nearly impossible—Hawkins had divided up his troops into three shifts. They'd fly fifty miles south—the course was actually more like seventy-five miles, because of two jogs to avoid possible Iraqi encampments. A Pave-Low would be waiting to meet them there. It had better be, since at best they had exactly enough fuel left to get there and no farther. Klee didn't want to risk detection by sending the large Air Force Special Operations helicopter directly to the base.

"Begging your pardon, sir, and no disrespect," said Rosen, who unlike some of his men sounded as if she meant the words when she said them. "But it would make better sense if I flew with the helicopters the whole time. Something goes wrong, I'm the only one who can fix them. I'm worried about Two. Slim Jim and me just curled the wires together in that harness. I mean, I can't guarantee they'll hold forever."

"Too risky," snapped Hawkins.

"Riskier than parachuting down here strapped to Captain Wong? Sir?"

Hawkins had to smile. Now *that* could have come from any of the troopers in his unit.

"You want to fly on every trip?" he asked her.

"I can work the weapons," Rosen said.

"Rosen, I'm going to marry you someday," he shouted as the helos came in.

7

Wong had managed to ease about ten feet closer to the rifle on the ground before the Iraqi captain returned with one of his men. Apparently they had been unable to find the rest of the team, though that did not convince the Iraqis that Wong was telling him the truth about being there alone.

"You may sit," the commander told him.

"I'd rather stand," said Wong.

"A stoic spy." His captor laughed. Then he said in Arabic that it would be wise for Wong to sit, or he would take out his pistol and shoot him without further warning.

Wong knew that it was another of the Iraqi captain's tests, this one designed to see if he spoke Arabic. He decided he would gain more by letting his captor think he had won the round.

"Why is it so important that I sit?" Wong asked in English.

"It's not important," replied the captain in Arabic. "If you wish to stand, then you will stand. Forever. Your sergeant, too."

Wong made no reply, but shifted his feet slightly, once again edging in the direction of his weapon. He was still a good five or six yards below the rocks where he'd put it.

The sun had gone behind the hill, and the ground where the weapon was lay in the shadows. That made it less likely the Iraqis would spot it, but it might also cost him a second or two locating it.

Wong wondered how long they would stay here. Perhaps until they gave up looking for the rest of the team.

Then what would they do? The easiest thing would be to execute him, though a self-admitted American spy had enormous value, even if he offered no tactical or strategic information. If they did not kill him, they would either relocate him immediately or go to a place where the captain would contact superiors for directions.

Beyond that, their specific course was impossible to predict but easily outlined. Information extraction was likely to be primitive but relatively effective. Wong's real value was not to the Iraqis but to the Russians, who would be highly interested in knowing exactly what he, and thus the Pentagon, actually knew about their weapons.

The captain had a cyanide implant in his leg near the groin; he would use it when and if appropriate. Until then, he would proceed with a hierarchical set of goals. Escape lay at the top of his grid, followed by destruction of the Scuds, and finally information-gathering about the Iraqi command and control structure, methods, and operations.

"So you see that you are checkmated," said the Iraqi, speaking again in English.

"An interesting choice of vocabulary," said Wong. "Do you play?"

"Chess? It happens that I do."

Wong nodded.

"Why is that of interest to you?"

"I am always looking for worthy opponents," said Wong.

The Iraqi captain made a snorting sound, then climbed back to the top of the hill, barely two feet from the rocks where the M-16 lay. Wong took the opportunity to sidle up another two steps. As he did he glanced at the Delta trooper captured with him. The sergeant gave him a half wink, showing that he knew what Wong was up to.

"I am beginning to think that you were telling the truth about coming alone," said the captain, turning around.

"There is little sense in lying," said Wong. "When precisely do you plan on killing me?"

"Would I kill a fellow grand master?" The Iraqi's clean-shaven lip was well suited to ironic grins, turning itself up and outward at the corner.

"I am hardly a grand master," said Wong. "My rating is merely 1900."

"And I a bare hundred points higher," said the Iraqi. The quickness of his response betrayed the fact that he was padding his rating—unlike Wong, who'd subtracted a thousand points.

"It's a pity that we don't have a board," said Wong.

"Yes, since we will be here for some while."

Why? Wong wondered. To prevent Wong from observing the Scuds? But that would mean they would be walking down the hillside in the dark, a time when it would be easier for the prisoners to escape.

What of that earlier reference to "who" rather than "what"? Surely the Iraqi knew English too well to confuse his pronouns. And what of the curious identity of his unit? The men were all obviously well trained, but were clearly not Republican Guards. Perhaps the chemical-warhead Scuds had been given to even more elite special units?

"You may sit, Sergeant," the Iraqi told the com specialist.

"I will stand with my captain, sir."

The Iraqi took out his pistol. Wong edged another step up the hill toward the M-16.

He couldn't see it, but the rock was at least four yards away. Two and a half steps, a full second and a half. Add another to pick up the rifle or even to kick it, get the grenade to go off.

Three seconds, optimistically. The sergeant would be dead and so would he.

"You may sit, Sergeant," Wong told him.

"No—*you* sit, Captain," said the Iraqi. "And only you. I'm not sure why you want to stand, but I want you to sit. Or your man will die."

The Delta trooper straightened, a calm air rising with his spine. He intended to die enshrouded with honor.

No need for that now. Not yet.

"We will both sit, then," said Wong. He bent slowly and then, as if losing his balance, fell over into the dirt.

Another yard and a half.

The barrel of a pistol slammed hard into his cheekbone as he rose.

"You will stop flailing around," said the captain, leaning so close Wong was nearly suffocated by the stale scent of his breath. "Or the next movement you make will be your last."

As if to underline his statement, an automatic rifle began firing in the distance, somewhere down the hillside.

8

As Dixon dove into the dirt, the woman in the doorway of the house began to spin. For a moment she was a ballerina, performing an unworldly dance. She was an angel, fluttering on a stage, a frenetic whirl.

Then she became a person again, then a body falling forward into the dirt.

By the time her face smashed into the ground, Dixon had lifted the barrel of his gun from the dirt and aimed at a figure coming around the left-hand corner of the building. He emptied the entire clip at the thick shadow, firing even as the shadow crumpled and fell off to the side. When his gun clicked empty, he grabbed for a fresh clip and at the same time began sliding back toward the dilapidated plow, a few yards away.

He could hear shouts as he reloaded. There were at least

two Iraqis at the back of the house, maybe more inside. He huddled behind the plow, prone, rifle next to the blackened blade.

Nothing.

The dogs were quiet. Probably they'd been shot when the woman was.

How many Iraqis were there? Two? Three? Enough to outflank him, certainly. Enough to rush him from different directions.

Kill him easily here. He was better off taking it to them. Get close to the building, hope to catch them by surprise.

Dixon jumped up and ran to the corner of the house where the dead soldier lay. A clip fell off his belt but he didn't stop for it, sliding in against the hard front of the house, crunching downward to look around the corner.

Nothing.

He heard something behind him, spun.

Nothing.

The woman lay a few feet away in the dirt. Dixon began to slide along the ground on one knee, inching along the rough front wall toward her. As he approached he saw a shadow edge against the doorway.

He froze, watching as an Iraqi in fresh, tan fatigues slowly emerged in a crouch, gun aimed toward the opposite hill. He had a clean-shaven face and no insignia on his uniform; his combat boots were black and shiny, as if they'd been polished that morning.

Dixon must have stared at him for four or five seconds before realizing he had a clean shot.

His first bullet missed. The man jerked his head around, stunned by the next five rounds. His chest and shoulder percolated with small explosions as he tried to straighten.

Dixon jumped up, firing a last burst to finish him as another soldier came around the far corner of the building. He lifted the AK-47 toward the new target, the stream of bullets dancing in the dirt and then up through the second man's leg and torso and face. Dixon saw the pain and then the body giving way, the man rolling backward. He saw the pain and then the death rattle and then the relief as the man died.

Or he thought he saw it. Dixon took a step, realized the first man was still moving in the doorway, right next to him. He pulled his rifle back and fired into his head point-blank, except that he didn't—the clip was gone. He froze, staring at the AK-47 in the man's hand, watching as the Iraqi struggled to raise it. He got it about two inches off the ground, grimacing, willing himself to fire, but he had no strength left, not even enough for vengeance. Slowly, the Iraqi lost the battle, the rifle sinking to the floor as his eyes rolled in his head. A faint odor of aftershave wafted up from the body as Dixon stared down at him.

If there had been any other soldiers, Dixon would have been an easy target, framed by the doorway, rifle empty and hanging down from his hand. Finally, he turned and walked back to the clip he had dropped, stooping deliberately, placing, not shoving, the fresh ammunition into the gun. Then he went to the woman.

He didn't have to lean over to know she was dead. Blood soaked her dress; her eyes were agape, staring at the corner of the house.

She was in her twenties, no older than he.

The Iraqis had killed her, not him. But he felt guilty somehow, as if he had pulled the trigger when she came out of the house.

"I have to do whatever it takes," he told himself aloud. "There are no civilians. There are no civilians. It's me or them."

But even as he turned to go into the house, he knew the words were lies. He couldn't change who he was, even if he could manage to do what duty told him he had to do.

As he stepped over the dead soldier in the small room at the front of the house, he thought he heard something in the next room. He threw himself to the floor, rolling and crashing against the leg of a wooden table, sending it into the wall.

He was in a kitchen. A pot of vegetable stew or something similar percolated on the primitive stove.

Food.

He jumped to his feet, grabbed the pot then yelled as it burned his hand. It splattered over the small gas jet, putting out the fire; the pot fell to the floor and he went down after it, spooning the hot mush out with his hands. His mouth and throat burned but his hunger forced him on, forced him to gulp it down. He couldn't tell what it tasted like, had no idea what it might be, knew only that it was food and he was starving.

He'd eaten halfway through the pot when he heard the noise from the other room. A creak, followed by a crack.

Someone sneaking up on him.

He could escape, run away.

He'd be pursued.

He pointed his AK-47 at the doorway. Slowly, Dixon slid his knee forward, edging around the leg of the table. He leaned his torso down, the gun's stock close to his ribs.

The view into the room was blocked off by an overturned chair. A trunk or large box sat beyond it.

Probably a bedroom.

Dixon slid to his stomach and began crawling. The smeared food on his finger made the trigger feel sticky. The place smelled of dirt and something sweet.

He reached the doorway. Curling his legs beneath him, Dixon shouldered against the jam and edged upward. Then he jumped full into the room, leaning on the trigger, sweeping across. An open door led to the backyard, where he could see the bodies of the two dogs lying in the dirt. He pushed his head to the side, looking out the window at the empty hillside and its low brush, then scanning the small room slowly.

Nothing.

No, something, on the floor beyond the bed.

Crying.

He jumped up onto the rope mattress, lost his balance, fell back.

A boy no older than two raised his head, wide brown eyes staring at him. The child began to babble, but didn't move.

Dixon pulled the gun back. He went back to the kitchen, grabbed the pot, and found a spoon. He shoveled food into a small plate he'd found on the floor, then walked with it back to the bedroom, setting it down in front of the toddler. The kid darted forward with a smile and began spooning the food into its mouth.

In twenty years, less, the kid would be a soldier. He'd be the enemy.

Better to kill him now. It might even be merciful—if no one found him within a few days, he would surely die.

Dixon stared at the little boy gobbling the food. There was no way he could harm him, no matter the circumstances. And yet he knew he had just done the boy irreparable harm, helped deprive him of his mother. Twenty years from now the kid would hate all Americans, and why not? An American had killed his mother.

Even if he knew the truth of what happened, he'd see it that way. He'd be right.

There was a sound from the roadway, a truck or a car. Dixon jerked his head toward the front of the house as the vehicle braked to a halt. He grabbed his gun and for a second thought of going to the front of the house. But that would be suicidal.

He thought, too, that he might take the boy with him—a stupid thought, gone in the instant it occurred to him.

He pushed up and jumped through the open back door, gripping the AK-47 and running up the hill.

He was about a third of the way to the top when the house exploded in flame.

9

Rosen jumped down from the weapons spar on Apache Two and gave the helicopter a good-luck pat. Then she took a few steps back, admiring the small black hulks in the dimming twilight. The Little Birds were all muscle, nothing wasted for show or ostentation; what you saw was what you got. She liked that. And what she saw now were two helos about as ready as they would ever be.

Rosen was not an expert on AH-6s; she hadn't a clue about bolt tolerances or even routine maintenance items, like when or even if the hydraulic lines should be flushed and tested. But the two helos were working, and that answered the number-one rule of technicians the world over: Ain't Broke, Don't Fix. Routine maintenance and touch-ups would have to wait until the helicopters returned south.

Actually, they needed more than touch-ups, Apache Two

in particular. Gashes and dents covered the sheet metal; a large crack and several bullet holes decorated the cockpit bubble. But the rotor and motor were intact and the wires she had field-stripped and twisted together at the start of this insanely long day were holding. She was good to go.

Or wait, since there was no sense leaving until the Pave-Low was en route to meet them. They weren't taking off for another hour and a half.

The wind kicked up; the sand felt like sleet in her face. With nothing left to do, Rosen went back to the bunker and took out her notebook again, thumbing past the page she'd filled earlier.

It did no good to brood on the past. Her grandma told her that a million times, raising her. So forget about Lieutenant Dixon. BJ. For now at least.

She turned her pen in her hand, thinking what she might write about. Some of the characters she worked with.

The pilots. What a bunch.

Shotgun:

I guess every unit has its own one-of-a-kind pilot type. Well, Shotgun—aka Captain O'Rourke—is one of a kind for the whole Air Force. He's probably unique in the world.

I don't know how he flies, but he must be pretty good because he always gets the tough assignments. And Sergeant Clyston says he's pretty good, which is praise right there.

But the thing about Shotgun is—he's like a walking junk-food store. He's always eating candy or Big Macs or something. And I mean always—you should

*see the crumbs on the floor of his airplane. He drinks
coffee while he's flying. I know because I've seen the
coffee stains!*

*I don't know how he manages it. I mean, the Hogs
aren't exactly 747s.*

She stopped. She was going to add that the A-10As
didn't have automatic pilots, but that was the kind of information that could conceivably help the enemy. So she went
on to other pilots.

Captain Glenon:

*Everybody calls him "Doberman." He probably
got the name because of his bark—he has a pretty
sharp temper and is very impatient. On the other
hand, he's been very nice and professional to me.*

*Maybe the best pilot in the bunch. Supposed to be
the best at using the Mavericks and dropping bombs,
but I'm not sure how you measure that exactly.
They're all pretty good here.*

*Nice guy. If I had had a brother, the kind of guy I'd
want him to be.*

Captain Hawkins:

*Macho Spec Ops Army captain. Okay for an offi-
cer, because all he wants is for you to do your job.
Likes to drink tea. Earl Grey tea.*

Rosen put her pen down and reread her notes. They were
bare descriptions, nothing that really would tell anybody
who these men were. Brave. Good pilots. Decent men.
Wasn't everybody?

No, no way. If you watched the movies or TV, sure—everybody was brave on television, everybody always did the right thing. War, life, weren't really like that.

If she was going to write a book about her experiences, if she was even going to write a journal, that was what she had to get down.

Her fingers had cramped with the cold. She brought them to her mouth and blew on them as she thought about how difficult it was to communicate what really went on.

Would anyone really want to know?

Sure, they would. The problem was, a lot of what really happened was boring. You got up, you pulled an antenna off a Hog because it was nicked by shrapnel, put a new one in. That was your day.

Boring. Important as all hell, but boring.

Even if you were doing it in Iraq, a hundred miles from any sizable allied force, closer to Baghdad than Oz. Even if any second an enemy artillery shell or a Scud could wipe you out.

You didn't think about that part. Not that you escaped it, exactly: you carried it around in your tool kit along with the wrenches and Mr. Persuasion, the extra-large ballpeen hammer at the bottom of the bag. It weighed the case down but you couldn't get rid of it.

She started writing again.

> *I can't get BJ out of my mind. He was such an innocent kid. Captain Glenon said he didn't even curse when he was first assigned to Devil Squadron, and probably hadn't had more than three beers in his life. A true fact. He was tall for a Hog driver, over six feet,*

with brushy blond hair and movie-star eyes. Real blue. He looked strong.

But innocent. Like a baby, almost. His lips were so soft.

Why do the good ones die first? Why is innocence the first victim?

PART THREE

HOG RULES

1

Doberman checked the numbers on his INS and glanced back at the map. He ought to be turning cartwheels over Al-Kajuk in about twenty minutes.

Seventeen minutes and thirty seconds, to be exact.

He ran through his instrument checks and scanned the sky for boogies. His biggest enemy, though, was impatience.

There were certain tricks—straining the throttle with your eyes, leaning on your seat restraints to pull her along—but the bottom line was that Hogs could not go fast. They also really, truly, did not like to fly high. Doberman's mount had groaned and grunted all the way to 18,500 feet, even though he promised to put the extra altitude to good use on the business end of the trip. She was built like a tank and wanted to act that way; she seemed to whine with displeasure when Doberman didn't turn in the direction of the thunderhead of flak at twelve thousand feet two miles off her right wing.

Judging from the altitude and spread of the flak cloud, Doberman figured the exploding bullets came from two or three ZSU-57-2 self-propelled antiaircraft guns, unguided by radar—though that didn't make the monster shells any less deadly. The site wasn't marked on the map. Doberman jotted the location down, just in case he still had some bombs left on the way home.

At precisely fifteen minutes from target, Doberman checked in with the AWACS controller tasked with coordinating support for the Apache mission. The crews rotated but he recognized the controller's Carolina accent from earlier as the specialist acknowledged Devil One's position.

The controller surprised him by saying that Wong hadn't called in a strike—or even come back on the air in the past hour.

"No contact?" he asked.

"Negative, Devil One. We are out of contact with the fire team at this time."

Out of contact?

"You're aware they're tracking Scuds," he said, more a statement than a question.

"Copy that. We have two Vipers en route to that kill box," said the controller. "We have a rotary asset en route, call sign Dark Snake. He is crossing north now. He may require assistance communicating with Apache Fire Team. We were told not to expect y'all," added the controller. "But we're happy to have ya."

"Roger that."

Doberman laid out the situation in his head. Dark Snake was the Spec Ops Pave Hawk, a specially modified Blackhawk designed for covert missions. Detailed to pick up Wong and the boys, the MH-60 would travel very close to the weeds, maybe only six feet off the ground, guided by special radar and other equipment. Because it was so low, it could have difficulty communicating with the ground team until it was almost on top of them. Doberman, much higher, could help out by establishing contact with the team and the helicopter individually. Then he'd relay messages back and forth like a telegraph operator in the Old West.

The Vipers were all-purpose F-16 fighter-bombers, most likely carrying dumb bombs and air-to-air missiles. The kill box was an arbitrary grid in the sky that included Al-Kajuk; the F-16s would be tasked to stand by until needed. Unlike the Hog, the pointy noses could fight off enemy interceptors, if any were so foolish as to appear. And unlike the Hog, they'd been designed to fly this far behind enemy lines.

What Doberman couldn't puzzle out was why Wong hadn't contacted the AWACS, at least to update the situation. But the controller didn't seem too concerned.

Bottom line: Wong would have called in if the erector had moved or if the Scuds had appeared. So Doberman should just go on in and take out the erector in the bombshelter hideaway under the road. Blow it up and the missiles in the mosque were useless.

No, they'd still be important targets—Saddam could turn this little party into World War III with them. But the erector was his priority target.

Piece of cake with the Mavericks—he could launch both and never get close to the SAMs.

Take out the erector, go for the SA-9s with the cluster bombs. Wouldn't want the pointy noses getting hurt when they came in to admire his handiwork.

2

Wong touched his thumbs to his pinkies, then his ring fingers, then the others, again and again, controlling his breathing as he did. He'd begun the meditational exercise when he first heard the AK-47s below. It helped him maintain his poise, but it did not change the basic calculus of the situation: since there had been no answering fire by M-16s or MP-5s, he had to assume the worst. The three remaining Delta troopers had been ambushed and were dead. He and the sergeant kneeling on the ground nearby were on their own.

They were guarded now only by the Iraqi captain and one soldier. The others had gone to investigate the gunfire. The Iraqi commander surely recognized that the gunfire had come from Russian-made weapons, but he did not exhibit overconfidence, keeping his pistol trained on Wong the whole time. If nothing else, his enemy's endurance was admirable.

The sun was at the horizon. The Scuds would be moving soon.

Captain Glennon would undoubtedly be on his way back. But a lone A-10A faced difficult odds against the SAM batteries, especially if Wong were not available to offer guidance.

Given the circumstances, it was time for a gambit.

"I wonder," Wong asked the Iraqi captain, "if you would care to play chess."

"Chess?"

"Why not?" said Wong. "I assume that we are not going anywhere for the time being."

"I don't see a chess set."

"Pawn to queen four," said Wong, giving the standard nomenclature for a timeworn opening move. It pushed the pawn in front of the white queen ahead two squares.

The captain laughed. "Thank you, no."

"Perhaps you prefer white," offered Wong. He nodded, as if sizing up the Iraqi. "You do seem like someone who would seize the initiative."

"You think that you could play an entire game out in your head?"

"You couldn't?"

The sharpness of his tone brought the desired response.

"Pawn to king's four," snapped the Iraqi.

"Queen's bishop four," replied Wong, pushing a pawn out in front of his bishop.

Within three moves, he was well embarked on a Sicilian defense; he set his bishop on move six, castled on seven, and spotted his knight boldly on the eighth—the modern

Dragon variation, an aggressive though tricky defense that sought to turn the initiative to black.

The Iraqi competently met the attack, though he hesitated over the moves, his eyes burrowing into the ground as he considered the board. Wong studied his clean-shaven chin, trying to add the accent and mannerisms into a profile. The man and his squad were obviously not Muslims, and were just as obviously members of an elite unit. That surely limited the possibilities.

A bodyguard unit?

For whom?

Wong took a step to the left, contemplating the possibilities and appalled by his severe lack of knowledge regarding the Iraqi order of battle. It was a deficiency that would have to be rectified when he escaped.

As he was now confident he would do, for he could see the butt end of his M-16 in the shadow next to the rock.

"Where are you going?" snapped the Iraqi captain.

"Oh, I beg your pardon," Wong said contritely. "I have a tendency to move around as I think. The combinations beyond this point are complex."

"You've obviously played this opening many times," said the man dryly.

"That's why the next move is difficult," said Wong. "Did you play very much in America?"

"I will play chess with you to amuse myself," said the Iraqi. "But I will not be drawn into conversation."

"Not even with a spy?" Wong glanced toward the Delta Force sergeant, who was sitting on the ground with his knees up. His fingers were curled together against his kneecaps. Wong hoped that the man had a concealed weapon in one of his boots or taped to a leg; that would, after all, be the Delta way.

But no matter. It was enough now that the sergeant caught his glance.

"I realize that you are contemplating a trick," said the Iraqi captain.

"Absolutely," said Wong cheerfully. "I'm working for a pawn advantage. Properly played, the Sicilian defense allows—"

"Not in the chess game. Why do you think you're so much more intelligent than I am? Why are Americans so arrogant?"

Wong might have made any number of replies, starting with the fact that he was not arrogant, merely naturally gifted, but before he could speak he heard a truck motor from the village side of the hill. He couldn't be sure it was a Scud carrier—the odds were probably against it—but he had to assume it was.

In the next second he heard something else: an explosion at the foot of the hill, a quarter of a mile away, maybe less. The Iraqi captain turned his head in that direction.

"Knight takes pawn—check," shouted Wong, diving for the gun.

3

Dixon heard the commotion as he ran up the hill. It was a distant, disorienting dream—American voices playing chess, then shouting, then gunshots. The house flamed below; he fell forward like a soul tossed from the swirl of hell, momentarily removed from the raging torment. He rolled over to his back, then to his stomach, realizing one of the voices was familiar—he grabbed at his rifle, trying to aim it to fire, but saw nothing. There was a loud thud behind him, near the house—it was the thud of a light cannon, pumping a second shell into the ruined house. Dixon saw three or four rocks to his right; he pushed himself there on his elbows, dragging his gun and his legs. For a moment he worried about being captured, then he felt his lungs cough with the dirt of the hill, choking. He got behind the rocks and then saw a branch a few yards below, a large, broken trunk that offered better protection—he jumped up and ran to it, surprised when he made it without being shot. It seemed to him that he was surrounded, that bullets were flying everywhere.

He thought of the woman in the house. The baby.

Had it died because he left the burner on the stove on?

Had it even been a gas stove? Dixon couldn't see it now—propane, gas? Or an old woodstove, the kind his mother used to talk about?

Why was he thinking about his mother? The hill below him shook again. The Iraqis had an armored vehicle or a light tank, and were firing its gun into the remains of the building.

His mother ran from the smoldering ruins, waving her hands, trying to stop him.

He pushed his rifle over the tree, trying to clear his head.

Dixon realized as his hands touched the bark that it wasn't a tree at all. He was huddled against the corpses of two dead Iraqi soldiers.

4

The M203 attached to the M-16 did not have a hairpin trigger, and it took more than a heavy jostle to set it off. What it really took was a good pull on the trigger, but Wong couldn't manage to slip his fingers there as he rolled. His hands flew around desperately, the ground shaking with a thud as a second shell hit the base of the hill in the distance. Finally, the grenade flashed from the weapon; Wong rolled from his back as the pudgy 40mm charge sailed square into the Iraqi commander's face, knocking him off balance as he began firing his pistol. The grenade ricocheted down the hill, exploding too far away to do any good—luckily for Wong, since any explosion this close would have killed him as well as his enemies. The Iraqi fell back, his gun flying with him. Someone shouted and now Wong had the rifle under control, cutting down the man in front of the Delta trooper who'd been captured with him. He slid around, unsure where the Iraqi commander was and confused by the gunfire at the base of the hill. Seeing the sergeant grabbing for the Iraqi's rifle, Wong ran to the top of the hill, spotting a knot of Iraqis. He flicked the rifle onto full automatic, peppering the three figures from the side. A shadow opposite the Iraqis jumped up; Wong realized it must be one of the missing members of his team. He could see something moving on the road directly below—three long tractor-trailers carrying tarped cylindrical payloads.

Scuds.

There was a pickup and then three canvas-backed military vehicles.

A burst of submachine-gun fire to his right sent him to the ground. He scooted to the crest and peered down. Two figures were climbing the clear hill; he barely caught himself from sending a burst through Sergeant Golden's chest, spotting the trooper's chocolate chip fatigues at twenty yards.

The other side of the hill shook with a fresh round, something from a light tank.

The priority now was the Satcom—Wong turned to find it but instead felt the long, thin edge of a combat knife slide up against the side of his neck. The meaty curve rested atop the sternohyoid and sternothyroid muscles—not the placement he would have made, but nonetheless arresting.

"Rook takes knight," hissed the Iraqi captain. "Checkmate."

"I think if you examine your position carefully," said Wong, shifting his weight to get a better balance on the slope, "you'll find it's a draw at best."

The Iraqi jerked the knife. It was so sharp that Wong

didn't feel the cut, though he realized blood had begun to flow.

"I think, Captain, that you overrate your strategy," said the Iraqi, twisting Wong around. "Stop," he yelled to the others, "or your captain will die."

The com specialist was stooped over the Satcom. The others on the hill were in the shadows and Wong couldn't tell if they'd been seen or even precisely where they were. The Iraqi commander pushed him to move right; he did so.

"Now, Captain," the Iraqi told Wong, "we will be going down the hill."

"As you wish," said Wong.

The Iraqi pressed his left shoulder into Wong's, forcing him forward, only to jerk the knife nervously against his neck. It would take considerable pressure to sever the artery or windpipe. In Wong's experience, the position was overrated as a lethal hold; it was difficult to properly leverage the arm so close to the intended victim.

On the other hand, escaping it was not necessarily easy. Especially since he had to do so quickly—the Spec Ops troops could hardly be expected to value Wong's life over their mission. Undoubtedly they were waiting for a good shot, even if it meant taking out Wong as well as the Iraqi.

"Excuse me," said Wong, stopping momentarily. The Iraqi pushed hard against him and jerked the knife to the top of his chin.

Perfect.

"No tricks," hissed the man.

"I was wondering if I might answer a call of nature," Wong told him.

"No!" shouted the man, and as he did he pushed the knife hard against Wong's throat, intending to intimidate him.

But this was just what Wong wished. The Iraqi's legs were too close to his. As his weight shifted with the knife, Wong added to it, jerking his upper body into his captor's and throwing both of them off balance. They fell in a tumble. He pivoted and smashed an elbow into the man's ribs as they swirled over. The knife jammed into Wong's jaw. Wong could not turn himself into his opponent fast enough to escape a second stab, but he managed to duck far enough so that it fell on his shoulder. In the meantime he pumped two quick jabs of his fist into the man's face; the Iraqi lost his grip on the knife and it clattered away as they fell into the dirt. The Iraqi captain managed a hard punch to Wong's nose. He felt the snap and knew it had been broken.

That made him mad.

Wong reared back and slammed the top of his skull into the Iraqi's forehead. The universe swirled and Wong thrashed his arms in every direction, raging as a thick flow of lava poured over him. He flailed and he writhed, and there was no longer one Iraqi but a dozen, all with knives and brass knuckles, pummeling him. He bulled his way through them, elbows, knees, feet, fists, head punching until finally he found his way to the surface of the inferno; with one last burst of energy he broke the molten iron bands holding his head back and staggered free, collapsing into the dirt.

He opened his eyes to see Golden's worried face hanging over him.

"Shit, Wong—you okay?"

Wong pulled himself up as if doing a controlled sit-up. Without checking his other wounds, he reached to his pants leg and tore off a piece of material, then held it to the long cut at his jaw. Had he cared to, he could have felt bone inside.

"Wong? You in shock?"

"I am not in shock," he told the sergeant calmly.

"You killed the fucker with your bare hands," Golden told him. "You snapped his neck."

"That is unfortunate," said Wong. "He might have supplied us with considerable information. I apologize for losing my temper."

Wong stood. His nose was bleeding as well as off-kilter. It stung, obviously broken, but was not a serious injury. There were various cuts and bruises on his body; the slash at his jaw was the worst. As long as he stopped the bleeding and did not get it infected, it would not be life-threatening.

"You're lucky to be alive," Golden told him.

"A clumsy escape, granted," said Wong. "But within acceptable margins."

"Margins like hell," said the sergeant. "Lou was going to plunk you in about two seconds."

Golden nodded at one of his men a few feet away. Wong merely shrugged and walked toward the Satcom.

"We had best get the attack under way," he said. "Captain Glenon will have returned by now, though he is undoubtedly too high for us to hear. He is notoriously impatient and ill-tempered."

"Company!" yelped one of the team members from the direction where the heavy-caliber weapon had been shaking the hill. "We have an armored car and two tanks coming up behind it now. Shit. T-62 mothers, and I'm looking at a platoon of Iraqis running up behind them."

5

Doberman swung back to the north, hunting through the blur of shadows for the highway and culvert. It was his second orbit south of the target area, but he still had trouble getting his bearings, let alone finding what he wanted to hit. Between his altitude—he was a nudge over twelve thousand feet—and the twilight, most of what he saw looked like light chocolate and dark mud.

Ten more minutes and there'd be only dark mud. The infrared seeker in his Maverick could be used as a primitive night-vision device, but the small angle on the viewer made it at least helpful to narrow the general area down before trying to find the target. Doberman's normally excellent eyes weren't cooperating; between the shadows and his fatigue, he wasn't even sure he had the highway. What he thought was the highway jagged to the right, which didn't seem right. He angled the Hog, nearing the northernmost edge of the circle he was drawing before he happened to glance to the left and saw a tiny brown brick at the left corner of his windscreen. He lost it as he began to turn, but he realized it must be the mobile SAM launcher.

Banking, Doberman quickly reoriented himself. And now the shadows had meaning—there was the village, there was the hill. He had the highway, knew where the SA-9s would be. He mapped out a long, wide loop that would give him an easy approach toward the culvert where the Scud erector was hidden.

Be nice to hear from Wong about now. He'd tried twice already without getting an answer.

"Devil One to Snake Eaters," he said, pushing his mike button in. "Yo, Wong, what's the story? Come on—you up or what?"

Doberman took his eyes off the windscreen to double-check the frequency and repeat the call.

Nada.

Dark Snake—the Blackhawk that was supposed to be rendezvousing with the team—didn't answer his hail either.

He came around at the southern end of his orbit, swinging into the approach. He was at nine thousand feet, roughly ten miles south of the culvert, lined up for a direct shot in. At twelve thousand feet, the Mavericks were accurate to roughly ten miles; the closer he got, the better his odds of hitting the target. The SA-9s protecting the culvert and launcher had a range of about five miles at that altitude; that left him with a perfectly safe firing envelope of just under a minute, plenty of time to take two shots under ordinary circumstances.

But that would mean attacking the SAMs with the cluster bombs. Tricky in the dark.

Better to fire just one Maverick at the launcher. He'd circle back, make sure he hit. If so, he could dial up one of the SA-9s on the TV screen, blow it to smithereens. He'd then have the option of using the cluster bombs on the last launcher, or letting the F-16s worry about it.

Nice to hear from Wong about now.

Gravity tickled his side as he righted the Hog and slotted into the attack run. Doberman saw a flash of light on the ground off his left wing, knew that meant the fire team was in trouble. But it was too late now—he pushed his head down into the Maverick monitor, easing the cursor toward the big shadow at the very corner of his screen. He waited for the shadow to move toward him—it was Zen, these final seconds, or maybe yin and yang, the target moving and the cursor moving, coming toward each other. It could be described by a mathematical formula: $A \times B = \text{boom}$.

He had the dark spot under the highway, the cursor was there. His thumb moved over the trigger.

"Bing-bang-boom," he said aloud, pushing the Maverick off from beneath his wing. The thick cylinder slipped downward, its blunt nose locked on the target. For a moment it stood in the air, propelled only by forward momentum, still part of the airplane. Then the Thiokol solid-fuel rocket caught with a throaty roar; the missile flashed away, bobbing up briefly before setting her teeth to the job at hand.

Doberman pulled off, heart pumping. He saw another flash in the shadow of the hill—something big was firing down there.

He had to make sure the erector was down. That was his priority.

There were more trucks, something moving on the road. Too much.

He took a hard breath, focusing his attention as he snapped the jet back into the attack path. He pushed his whole body down to the right, as if he wanted to ram the video screen with his head. He slipped the Maverick's aim point down and saw smoke lingering from the first missile hit.

Nailed the sucker. The culvert had been replaced by an immense crater.

He began hunting for the SAM launcher at the close end of the highway. He found it, lost it, then pulled off, realizing he was at the edge of his safety margin.

He banked south, intending to turn to the east and come at the SA-9 from the other direction. He was just straightening out when he saw a long thick shadow several hundred yards south of the highway, in a cleared area to his left.

The Scud erector had been moved.

6

Wong repeated his message into the communications hand-set as the Iraqi tanks began firing. Behind him, two of the Delta team members peppered the slope with automatic fire and grenades.

"Devil One, this is Apache Fire Team Snake Eaters," Wong said. "Do you have your ears on?"

"Ears on? What the hell, Wong, you think you're talk-ing into a goddamn CB set?" responded Doberman. "Shit."

"I selected a vernacular sure to attract your attention," he replied. "You did not answer my first two calls."

"What calls? I've tried hailing you three or four times over the past ten minutes."

A fresh salvo of grenades exploded down the hill. The Iraqi tanks had so far missed very high, their shells sailing far over the hillside. Wong had no illusion, however, that this would continue indefinitely. Golden ran back and began tugging his sleeve—they had to move out.

"There are three Scud carriers en route to the erector site," Wong told Doberman quickly. "Do you copy?"

"I don't see the carriers but I have the erector. It's moved from the culvert. Are you under attack?"

"Immaterial," said Wong. "The Scuds are your priority."

"No shit. I'm going to vector in help. I see three tanks. Are you on the hill?"

"The SA-9s have a lethal envelope slightly beyond the published specifications that you may be aware of," said Wong calmly. "Recent alterations to the infrared seeker heads as well as some improvements in the rocket motor have increased their kill potential by a factor of one-point-five."

The hillside reverberated as the T-62s fired their 100mm guns nearly simultaneously. Their charges slammed into the hillside below the American position. Golden lost his balance, grabbing Wong as he fell.

"We have to go," he said.

"Wong, there's a helo on its way," Doberman shouted. "Call sign—"

The rest of the transmission was swallowed by static.

"I'm afraid we're going to have to relocate," Wong told Doberman as the ground shook again. The Iraqis had once more missed, but their margin was much closer. Dirt and debris showered around him; Wong lost his balance and the headset, rolling against the rocks.

"Now!" shouted Golden, managing to get to his feet.

He told his men to cover the retreat with smoke grenades and move out. "Smoke! Smoke! Come on, Wong!"

Wong scooped up the satellite antenna and began dragging the Satcom rucksack down the hillside. He'd only taken two steps when he remembered that he hadn't searched the Iraqi captain. He threw down the dish and turned back.

"Where the hell are you going, Wong?" shouted Golden.

"Be right with you, Sergeant. Please take the Satcom and proceed without me," yelled Wong.

In the next moment a fresh set of salvos from the tanks rocked the hillside and Wong flew face first into the hill. The last member of the fire team slid past to the left. Wong pushed himself to his feet. The Iraqis were shouting below, their voices a cacophony of anguished cries and commands to attack. Wong began to choke; he put his arm to his face, using his sleeve as a makeshift filter. The Iraqi captain lay heaped over to his right, perhaps ten yards away. As he ran toward it, the tanks launched another set of salvos. While their rate of fire was admirable, their marksmanship left a lot to be desired, though not by Wong. He stumbled sideways down the hill a few feet, lost his balance, and fell onto the Iraqi captain's body. The thick cloud of soot and dirt made it impossible to see what he was doing; he had to feel for the pockets with his hands. He found a folded map or document and something else in one of the shirt flaps. That was going to have to suffice—he threw himself backward in the direction he'd come, rolling two or three yards downhill before managing to get his arm out and lever himself to his feet. He heard the sound of a tank shell whizzing by at close range and thought of the old saying about the bullet you heard was never the one that got you. There must be some truth to that, he realized, given the innate lag time involved in the speed of sound and the human aural apparatus.

In the next second, he found himself flying through the air, launched by an explosion he hadn't heard.

7

Gravity slapped Doberman hard in the head, punishing him for trying to do too many things at once. He struggled against the black tinge at the edge of his face, holding the hard maneuver and fighting the instinct that wanted him to ease off on the stick. He lost Wong's transmission in a tangle of static; saw all sorts of ground fire and had a warning on the RWR. Fighting off the confusion, he steadied his hand on the stick and put his eyes back on the Maverick video monitor, pasting them there as he waited for the long gray shadow of the missile erector to appear. Some kind of ground battery, probably on a mobile platform, began firing flak at him; black pebbles and white streaks dotted the video screen as well as the canopy above him.

No target.

Doberman began cursing. He pulled back on the stick,

starting to bank to his right. The long ladder materialized at the edge of his screen. It fuzzed, and for a moment he couldn't be sure whether he had his target or an optical illusion. He stayed on course and switched the Maverick into what passed for close-up mode, doubling the magnification but narrowing his range of vision by about the same percentage. The ladder morphed into a two-by-six with graffiti, then back into something approximating a construction crane half covered by a tarp. The crane portion was moving, swinging around slowly. Doberman steadied his small aiming cursor on the heart of the crane and let the missile go. He kept his eyes on the screen for another two or three seconds, locked on his target, entranced by the gray fuzz. Then he shook himself out of it and yanked the Hog around, hitting the diversionary flares. He assumed the SA-9s had launched and jinked hard right then back left, leaving the small flares out to suck their IR sensors away.

At least he hoped they would. He counted off twenty seconds, shucking and jiving the whole way, cutting corners in the sky before starting to reorient himself for another attack. The altimeter ladder told him he'd fallen to 8,050 feet. The CBUs—long suitcases of miniature antiarmor and personnel bombs—had been preset to be delivered from roughly eight thousand feet; he had to get higher to get a good angle before letting them go. He swung out of his bank and put his nose upward, now more than twelve miles from his target, well out of range of the missiles and flak. He could see large flashes near the hill on the left, in front of the village.

Wong's team, taking heavy fire. He'd have to try to help them, the SA-9s be damned.

"Devil One to Bro Leader," he said, trying to raise the

F-16s. There was no answer. Doberman angled to make his approach from the west, keeping as much distance as possible between himself and the SAMs until the last moment. He saw a flash off his right wing, then something moving on the ground farther along—maybe the Scuds.

Another set of muzzle flashes below the hill. If they kept that up, he'd have an easy time taking them out.

Couldn't use the CBUs—no telling how close the tanks were to Wong.

Have to mash them with the cannon.

Lower attack. Have to hurry, too. The bastards were flailing.

He tried the F-16s one last time. When the radio didn't snap back with pointy-nose slang, Doberman called the AWACS, asking for information on the Vipers and giving his position. In the meantime the Hog seemed to fly herself, homing in on the thick shadows at the base of the hill. He was nearly in range as his finger clicked off the talk button; his eyes separated the fresh muzzle flashes into real targets, thick and juicy. Doberman slammed the stick hard, pitching the Hog into the attack. A gray shroud filled his windshield, a cloud of dust or smoke or fog spewing from the hillside.

Come on, he thought. *Fire again you bastards. Show me where the hell you are.*

"Bro flight is zero-three from target," said the AWACS controller over the radio. Doberman lost the rest of the message as he struggled to find the tanks in the darkness. Something very bright flashed in the distance, back near the highway.

He was below four thousand feet and still didn't have a target. He had mud and crap and dirt and shit, but no target.

SA-9s on their way. That was what the flash was.

Three thousand feet. Shit. What the hell happened?

Two thousand. Too late now. Sorry, Wong.

He broke off, changing his plan as the Hog slid down into the mud, a thousand feet and still in a dive. He had a good view of the highway and saw a tower peeking out from the village—the minaret of the mosque, obviously— about eleven o'clock off his nose. A four-barreled ZSU-23 opened up near the edge of the village, its stream of bullets whipping for him. Doberman's brain went critical, leaping into full-blown Hog-driver mode; he dodged the stream of shells without thinking about them, hunkering in the A-10A's titanium bathtub while his eyes hunted for something to hit. He had a long shadow in the center of the roadway a quarter of a mile off. He couldn't tell what it was, but at this point it didn't matter. Thirty-millimeter slugs from the Hog's gun chewed into the thick brick, slicing it in two. There was no secondary explosion, however, and Doberman was by it before he could figure out what he'd hit. He banked hard, trying to cut a path low against the hill, away from the flak.

Dragged down by the four heavy cluster bombs on her wings, the Hog wallowed in the air, her energy robbed by the maneuvers and momentum.

He saw a flash from the corner of his eye. It was too big for tracers from the triple-A, but not big enough for the Scud.

The SA-9, closer than he thought, almost point-blank.

He rammed the stick in the opposite direction and slammed his hand against the button to fire off more decoy flares. But he'd already shot his wad; there was nothing but cold air between his engines and the heat-seeker gunning for him.

The plane rocked to the right, down to five hundred feet, starting to slide sideways despite her pilot's efforts to nose her around. Doberman felt something give way in his stomach, and he realized he'd pushed the line way too far tonight.

8

Dirt and pain pushed Wong's eyes closed as he fell into the ground. He seemed to fall right through the hill, through the rocks, into hell.

Curious. He would have thought he'd merit assignment to the other destination.

The ground rolled around him as he flailed. He heard the distinctive whine of a pair of A-10A turbofans above him and knew he hadn't died.

Yet.

His left eye stayed closed; he saw only haze with his right.

On his knees, he felt around him, waiting either to die or see. Dust flew in particles in front of his head. Stones. The ground.

He found two small stubs, felt them gently, pushed his face down into them as his right eye gained focus.

Two fingers.

He pulled his own hands to his face to make sure they weren't his. As he touched his left cheek a flame erupted there.

His hands were intact. He'd been shot in the face, or near the face. That was why he couldn't open his left eye.

Burned, not shot. A piece of a red-hot shrapnel had glanced off his cheekbone. He was extremely lucky—the same shell had obliterated the Iraqi captain's body; parts of the corpse were scattered around him. Wong's uniform was soaked with the dead man's blood.

An awful roar rent the air. The A-10A fired its cannon at a target on the highway. There was answering fire, explosions everywhere. Missiles and flames leaped into the air.

Perhaps this really *was* hell.

Wong worried that he had dropped the dead man's papers. He began hunting around on the ground in front of him, hands spread wide like a sunbather who'd lost a contact lens in the sand. Finally, he remembered he'd stuffed them in his pocket—he pounded his chest and found them there, or at least felt something he'd have to pretend were them for now. Still unable to see through his left eye, he heaved himself down the hill toward a large shadow. The figure waved its arms at him, beckoning.

Charon or Sergeant Golden, at this moment it made no difference. He found his balance and began running with all the strength he had left.

9

Until he'd come to the Gulf, Doberman hadn't believed in luck. In fact, he'd hated the idea. Trained as an engineer, he thought—he knew—that you could roll all that BS together—luck, ESP, UFOs, ghosts, angels, Santa Claus—and toss it into the trash heap. The world could be expressed mathematically, with cold numbers and complex equations. Things that appeared random actually occurred within predictable parameters, and no amount of superstition could change them.

But he sure as hell believed in luck now, or at least wanted to, ramming his body and hopefully the Hog to the southeast and as low as he could go, trying to get his nose pointed toward the SA-9s' IR sniffers. The idea wasn't as crazy as it seemed—the less of a heat signal he presented to the missiles, the harder it would be for them to find him.

They were galloping toward him at maybe Mach 1.5; he had all of a second and a half to complete his maneuver.

Doberman got his nose in the direction of the SAM launchers and turned the Hog over, goosing the CBUs from his wings as he did. The plane was far too low for the bombs to explode properly; he just wanted to get rid of the weight.

Except, one of them did explode. And while the air rumbled around him and sweat poured from every pore of his body, the SA-9 sucked in the sudden heat and dove for it.

Doberman felt something ping the rear fuselage, a sharp thud and shake, but his controls stayed solid and he was actually climbing. Tracers whizzed well overhead. The air buffeted worse than a hurricane. He saw light and thought he felt heat, and then found a large telephone pole moving on the road ahead of him. It took another second before he saw that the pole was laid out flat and realized it was a Scud carrier.

He had to pull back to get it into the aiming cue. The A-10A jerked her nose up and he fired, lead and uranium and blood flowing in a thick hose, splattering the ground and the air. He banked to his right, struggling to reorient himself in the peppery haze as the ground crackled with tracers and muzzle flashes.

The tanks were back on the other side of the hill. The SAM launchers were on his right; he was within range, but he guessed—he hoped—that they'd already shot their wad. He hustled the Hog to the west, trying to keep an eye on the bouncing shadows of black and red. The T-62s were still firing at Wong's team.

Doberman drew a long breath. You could build a ship with the flak in the air. Fortunately, the tracers were arcing high into the sky, the shells apparently set to explode far above. For all its fury, the triple-A was harmless.

Unless, of course, the bullets actually flew through the plane.

Doberman had a good mark on a tank. He pushed the Hog toward it, judging that he could cut left after firing and avoid the worst of the antiair. Three hundred feet above ground level, he came in on a T-62 turret as the tank's machine gun began to fire toward the top of the hill.

"See you in hell, you son of a bitch," said Doberman.

In the two seconds his finger stayed on the trigger, more than a hundred rounds spit from the front of the plane. The foot-long shells glowed in the dimness as they sped toward their target, ripping the highway and then the metal of the tank and then the ground beyond. Half a dozen of the 30mm warheads made their way through the hard metal of the tank, bouncing wildly in a ricochet of death through the cramped quarters of the thirty-six-ton tank.

By the time the last of the crew had died, Doberman had already trained the Hog's GAU-8/A Avenger cannon on a second target and begun to fire. His angle was poor, however, and he didn't have enough room to stay on the tank and not collide with the hill. He flicked off the gun and wagged his way clear for another run, cutting left and then flicking right to give the people firing at him less of a target.

And they *were* firing on him. He was at a hundred feet, barely higher than the hill. The Iraqis threw everything they had at him—antiaircraft guns, rifles, pistols, maybe even a knife or two.

No rational man would have turned back for another run.

But Captain Glenon wasn't rational. He was a Hog driver. And having come this far, he wasn't about to go home.

The Gatling mechanism began pumping beneath his seat as Doberman whipped back toward the hill and immediately found the tank front and center in his HUD aiming cue. He mashed the rudder pedals back and forth, lacing the top of the tank. Two swishes and the tank disappeared, steamed into oblivion.

Dark black spitballs arced past his windshield, spewed by an optically aimed ZSU-23 posted below the village. Doberman tucked his wing in and got the barrels sighted as they swung toward him. He rushed his shot, the enemy spitballs turning into footballs; he pushed hard on the stick, ramming his stream of bullets down into the target. His wings bounced up and down and he had a hard time putting the Hog where he wanted it to go, even though he didn't think he'd been hit. He leaned on the trigger and finally squashed the gun, saw parts of the treads and one of the barrels flying upward, but no more bullets. He pulled his right wing up, feeling his way back across the village, hugging the ground and looking for something big to shoot at.

Nothing. The antiair fire seemed to have exhausted itself. One of the tanks was on fire. He pulled up into the darkness away from the Iraqi positions, quickly scanning his instruments. His heart pounded so fast it sounded like a downpour on a tin roof.

At spec. Controls good. Steady climb.

He'd made it. And hell, he even had a good twenty minutes of fuel to spare.

He was one lucky SOB. A good pilot, maybe even great—but luckier than anyone had a right to be.

Doberman relaxed a little, shoulders sagging ever so

slightly as he leaned back against the Hog's ejector seat. His legs were cramping; he rocked his knees toward each other gently.

"Devil One, this is Bro Leader," said the leader of the F-16 two-ship. "Request you stand off while we attack."

"If you can find something standing down there to hit," Doberman told the late arrivers, "be my guest."

10

Dixon was pinned there, behind the bodies, by a flurry of machine-gun and heavy-weapons fire. The air boiled with explosions and metal and heat; flames flew in every direction and he had to hunker into the ground, barely aware of anything more than a foot away. He couldn't even get up to retrieve his AK-47, even though it lay on the side of the hill only a yard or two away. Every time he rose or crawled or leaned in its direction, the ground exploded with bullets.

He wasn't sure how long he stayed there, or why the Iraqis firing at him didn't just charge and get it over with. The machine gun seemed to be shooting from a good way off, though in the dark he couldn't really tell. Shells from a tank or artillery piece peppered the top of the hill, most landing well behind him; even so, they threw up fierce amounts of dirt and grit.

Dixon's lips pressed into the ground, waiting for something to happen. Images crowded at the corners of his brain, ghosts trying to haunt him—his mother, the first man he had killed at close range, the Iraqi woman caught in the cross fire below, the baby. He sat in a lifeboat in the middle of the ocean; the ghosts clawed the sides from the icy water, reaching for him, crying to be saved. But he knew that if he let one into the boat, if he even reached for one, it would be the end—Dixon himself would sink, swamped by their weight, dragged to his own death. He resisted; he closed his eyes against the tracers and the smoke and the shrapnel and the metal and the gunpowder and the death. He told himself that the Iraqis had killed the woman and her child, not him. He pushed his body close to the dead soldiers, protected by their freshly wasted bones. He slipped his sleeve over his mouth, trying to breathe the last air unpolluted by the hot winds of death that flowed over the battlefield.

One of the bodies before him began to move. It sprang up, laughing in his face, leering over him.

He fought it back down, forced his eyes to see that the man was truly dead.

The body collapsed as the foot of the hill exploded with a tumultuous hiss. The red flare of flames shot up toward the sky.

Dixon's body burned with the heat, though the fire was far away. He couldn't stand it any longer. He got to his knees, looming over the dead men, an easy target, not caring that he would soon be dead.

And then he heard a sound in the distance, a low, familiar *whump*—the exact sound a Blackhawk helicopter made as it flew. He heard it over everything, the explosions, the curses, the wails of wounded men. He heard it and he knew it was coming toward him.

And now he didn't know if the Iraqis were still firing or not, he didn't know if he was pursued by ghosts or bullets or bombs or corpses or curses. He knew only that he was on his feet and he was running, pushing toward the growing but still distant whomp of the helicopter, a heavy, continuous thud that drummed him full of hope.

11

By the time Wong reached the roadway, the four Delta troopers had set up the Satcom and were talking to the Blackhawk helicopter detailed to pick them up. The helo—technically an Air Force Special Operations MH-60G Pave Hawk, call sign Dark Snake—had located them with the aid of its FLIR imager and had a calculated ETA under forty-five seconds. The troopers could hear it but not see it; the southwest horizon was now a dark blur. Two F-16s were about to make a run on the Scuds.

"I suggest we request that the F-16s hold off their bombing run until we have egressed," Wong told Golden. "And in any event, it would be prudent to don our chemical gear."

Golden tapped the com specialist, indicating that he ought to follow the captain's suggestions. The rest of the men silently reached to their rucksacks, pulling out the moon gear.

Wong had lost his rucksack back on the hill, and thus had no NBC suit to put on. Instead, he pulled out the papers he'd taken from the Iraqi, examining them with the aid of a small penlight he borrowed from Golden.

One of the folded sheets contained two photos, both fairly battered. In one, an older Iraqi woman waved hesitantly. In the second, a younger version of the dead captain waved in front of a stairway to the Chicago El. The paper had some writing on it in Arabic; it was faded and difficult to read, but Wong guessed it was a personal letter or will of some type.

The other papers were two small sheets from a notebook. These had numbers as well as letters on them, instructions or map coordinates. There wasn't time to study them before the ground started whipping with grit thrown up by the helicopter's whirlies.

"Incoming!" shouted someone as the team began scrambling for the Pave Hawk.

A shell exploded at least fifty yards short of the highway. Tossed by either a mortar or the light armored vehicle that had harassed them back at the hill, it proved to be more inspiration than nemesis. The team bolted for the helicopter as one; Wong caught up and leaped through the wide-open door of the helo, colliding with the gunner as the helicopter pitched away. In nearly the same instant the F-16s launched their attack, pickling their two-thousand-ton Mk-84 iron bombs in an impressive send-off.

Wong rolled to his back and sat up, shaking his head as the helicopter's pilot slid into warp drive for home.

"What's wrong, Captain?" Golden asked. For the first

time since they had met, the sergeant actually seemed concerned and almost friendly.

Obviously an aberration, thought Wong.

"The aircraft tasked to strike the SS-1 or so-called Scud missiles were obviously early-model F-16s without precision weapons," Wong informed him. "Perhaps not as inappropriate as A-10A Thunderbolt IIs, but a bad match nonetheless. We can see evidence of this in the fact that they resorted to dropping Mk-84 bombs, which naturally will result in a tonnage-to-devastation ratio frighteningly close to that experienced in World War Two."

"What are you saying?"

"A pair of missiles at the lower, less expensive end of the Paveway series, or perhaps even the AGM-65s used by our friends in the Thunderbolt IIs, would have been the weapon of choice. Unless, of course, one belongs to the accounting branch."

"You think they missed?"

Wong chortled. "Hardly. We saw clear evidence presented by the numerous secondary explosions."

"So what's the big deal?"

Wong reached into his pocket for the Iraqi's notes without answering. People either understood efficiency or they didn't; there was no use explaining it.

Modified for covert and special operations, the MH-60G Pave Hawk began life at Sikorsky as a plain-Jane UH-60 Blackhawk, the muscular successor to the UH-1 Huey, arguably the most successful military utility helicopter of all time. Powered by a pair of General Electric T700-GE-401 turboshaft engines that were rated for 180 knots cruising speed, stock Blackhawks had a range of nearly 375 miles. All Pave Hawks, however, were rigged for extra internal fuel; this particular bird also carried two large 117-gallon tanks off her side, increasing not only her range but her ability to linger in the war zone. A long airborne refueling probe stuck out from her nose, making the craft look something like a medieval knight and horse rushing to battle. Mounted on each door was a .50-inch machine gun; pintle mounts for 7.62mm miniguns were set on the sliding forward cabin windows, though at the moment the posts weren't manned. The chopper's equipment set included FLIR or forward-looking infrared, ground-mapping (and weather-avoidance) radar, advanced INS and global positioning and com gear. While similar to the gear in the larger Pave-Lows, the avionics were not quite as advanced or powerful, though the difference would hardly be noticeable on most missions, including this Injun-country extraction. The men manning the craft were handpicked veterans, trained for a range of missions from rescue to covert action. Painted in a brown chocolate-chip scheme somewhat similar to the troopers' camo fatigues, the Blackhawk bore three white bands around the fuselage behind the cabin, a recognition code for Coalition forces.

Wong's Arabic was rusty and the captain's handwriting poor. Jostled in the tight cabin, he stared at the scribbles for two or three minutes before finally realizing that they were in code. Wong looked up suddenly, realizing that Golden was staring over his shoulder.

"What do you have?" asked the sergeant.

"The first sheet contains a set of coordinates which are useless without the map they refer to," said Wong. "But the second has hand-copied instructions, I believe. Can you decipher them?"

"Are you kidding?"

"No." Wong took the paper back without asking why everyone thought he was always playing the comedian. "Incidentally, your diversion proved useful, as it sent most of the Iraqi force away at an opportune time. How precisely did you acquire the AK-47?"

"What AK-47?"

"You did not fire near the northern base of the hill?"

"The north side? Hell no. We were in the village. We came back up the east slope. I didn't even know you'd been captured until the shooting started. *You* saved us, not the other way around."

"You were never on the northwestern side of the hill? Or on the ground there?"

Wong asked the question, though by now he realized that this was impossible. He reconsidered the battle, sorting it into its different components.

Wong rose slowly, grabbing one of the long belts at the side of the bird's cabin to steady himself as he passed forward. The helicopter's pilots sat at a pair of well-equipped consoles, separated by a wide console with more dials, buttons, and indicators than the average nuclear power plant.

"Excuse me," he said, bending across the central console. "I'd like to speak to the commander."

"Yo," said the pilot on the right.

"I will require immediate transportation to King Fahd Royal Air Base," said Wong.

"Uh, Captain, first of all, don't put your hand up there, all right? You're too damn close to the throttle."

Wong removed his hand without noting that it had been nowhere near the control in question.

"Thank you," said the pilot. "Now, as for King Fahd—that's where we're headed, assuming we cross ten million miles of SAMs, antiair guns, hostile troop positions, and rattlesnakes. I would appreciate it if you took a seat."

"Very good," said Wong. "Let me assure you that there are no known species of rattlesnakes in Iraq, or in Saudi Arabia for that matter. Indeed, they are a New World species exclusively."

"Ha-ha," said the pilot. "Very funny."

At a loss to understand why, Wong merely shrugged and went to the back.

12

Doberman hunched to the side of the cockpit, leaning over the throttle console as he tried to get a good view of the highway. Four British Tornadoes had been detailed by the AWACS controller to mop up; Doberman had been asked to play impromptu spotter for them, mapping out the site. The F-16s, meanwhile, were swinging south to shadow the Pave Hawk in case it got into trouble.

There were three or four good-sized fires going where the Vipers had dropped their bombs. Red and yellow mixed with a black smoke so dark and inky it stood out in the heavy twilight. Doberman leaned the Hog gently on her wing, fixing his eyes on the largest and nearest fire. It seemed to be a fuel truck, not a missile, though from six thousand feet, even in the daylight it would not be easy to tell. A second hulk farther along seemed definitely to be a missile; only the tractor cab was burning. He continued south, spotting three medium-sized shadows near where he'd hit the erector. They looked like the most likely targets, though he wasn't sure what they were.

He banked northward, making sure the SA-9 sites were smashed. The ground looked flat—no flames, no smoke, nothing. The Vipers had reported a hit on the remaining launcher and they looked to be correct—if there had been a live SAM launcher down there, Doberman would be swinging from a parachute.

"Devil One, hay-low Yank, this is Tory Leader. We are five klicks south of you and request target guidance."

"Yeah, One to Tory, hang tight," he told the British pilot, who was under thirty seconds away. "I got three trucks near the erector. Hang tight, I'm coming back low and slow to eyeball this mess."

Doberman lined up his weary Hog for one more walk-through. He pushed his nose toward the ground, coming over the highway toward the smashed tanks and hill in a straight-at-the-road dive, dropping his altitude below two thousand feet. There was an armored vehicle of some sort, smaller than a tank, at the corner of the hill beyond the T-62s he'd unzipped. He stayed with the road over the village, no longer drawing antiaircraft fire. The idiots had shot themselves dry.

Doberman felt his heartbeat picking up as he nosed closer to the road, down at a thousand feet now. It was low for a plane flying in the dark without ground-terrain radar, even though he knew the area pretty well. He arced toward the burning fuel truck, its flames flickering toward his hull. Two long cylinders lay in the dirt about a hundred yards away. One was definitely smashed—it looked like a broken crayon stomped into a carpet.

He couldn't be sure about the other. He steadied the plane, riding out to the erector south of the highway. One of the shadows he'd seen was clearly a tent; the other two were small panel vans.

Not much for the Tornadoes to hit, but that was their business. He gave Tory Leader a quick rundown, offering to mop up himself with his cannon while they went on to another target.

"Thanks, Yank, but we'll stay with this tea party all the same," said the British pilot cheerfully. "Our primary was scratched, which was why we were sent here. You Americans are putting on quite the show. Hogging all the glory, eh?"

The Englishman meant it as a joke and even something of a compliment, but it struck Doberman the wrong way. He punched the mike button, intending to snarl that nobody here was doing it for the goddamn glory. Nobody. He wanted to scream that he'd lost a squadron mate today, a good kid, to this bullshit, and worried that he'd lose more.

He didn't say it, though. For one of the few times in his life, Doberman controlled his temper and gave only a brief acknowledgment. Then he pumped the throttle and gave himself stick, setting course for the long and hazardous trip home.

13

Dixon heard the helicopter's engines whirl into high gear. He pushed himself to run faster, conscious now that salvation was within reach. He ran and he ran, long legs striding, lungs wrenching against his ribs, eyes scratching the dark night to make out the helo. Finally, he saw it, out ahead across the road, its dark hull stuttering, the rotor blades whirling. It seemed like a mirage.

It wasn't. It was real and it was less than a half mile away. He could feel the ground pounding with the heavy twin motors. He ran and he ran, forgetting his wounds and his hunger, his thirst and his fear, forgetting most of all his conscience and the ghosts.

And then he realized that the helicopter was moving, speeding away; already it was growing smaller, already it was too far to stop. He ran another few feet and launched himself, arms grabbing the empty air in despair, two hundred yards from being saved.

14

Sergeant Rosen strained against the seat restraints in the AH-6 Little Bird, watching the narrow fringe of reddish light at the horizon sift into blackness. The desert before her lay empty, its vastness turned from idea to fact. Something in the human imagination hated the void, made it feel cold; Rosen braced herself against the frame of the small helicopter and stared. She had seen a great deal in her life, raised by her grandparents and aunt in a rough neighborhood, working her way through all kinds of crap growing up and then in the military. But she had not understood the fierceness at the edge of the horizon until the war; she had not understood that every human soul had a hollow place inside, a pocket where it could go to survive.

A strong gust of wind smacked against the helo's bubble nose, whistling over the Allison turboshaft and its main rotor. Whipping over the desert at almost a hundred and fifty miles an hour, the crammed chopper drew a straight

line toward its rendezvous, skids less than six feet from the
sand. It was their third and next-to-last trip; only a half-
dozen troopers and their gear were left at Fort Apache now.

The Little Bird had first undergone trials as the Army
Defender light helicopter in 1963; christened the OH-6A
Cayuse, the chopper saw extensive duty in Vietnam as a
support and scout craft. The first production helicopter in
the U.S. to use a gas turbine engine, the OH-6 was fast and
maneuverable. It could sport a variety of weapons, starting
with the smallish but popular 7.62mm minigun and pro-
gressing right up to TOW missiles. The versatile design had
been enhanced several times after its introduction, proving
more versatile than craft two or three times more costly.

Rosen admired the simplicity of design. Despite the
high-tech cockpit with its fancy night-gear and radar, the
Spec Ops AH-6G melded design with function without ex-
cess. It was like a stripped '63 Chevy Nova, all engine and
drivetrain, no BS like leather or climate control. You
gunned it and you knew what you had.

"Sixty seconds to Sandlot," announced Fernandez, the
pilot. He turned his head slightly in Rosen's direction; he'd
donned night-vision goggles before taking off, and looked
more cyborg than human. Rosen turned back and looked
over her shoulder at the three Delta troopers crowded into
the back of the tiny helo; they all had heard and gave slight
nods.

She couldn't see the big Pave-Low they were meeting
until Fernandez whipped the tail around to pull the craft to
a landing. The pilot of the big bird had found a shallow de-
pression to sit in, waiting there patiently as the two AH-6s
ferried men and supplies from the clandestine fort roughly
forty miles away. The troopers in the back jumped from the

Little Bird even as it settled in near the big helicopter, no doubt glad to stretch their legs after the knee-crunching shuttle. They were the Pave-Low's last passengers; the Little Birds would return and top off by themselves from the tanks the Pave-Low had brought north for them. Then they'd zigzag across the border on their own.

"Okay," Rosen shouted to Fernandez as the others got out. "Let me check the wires again." The jury-rigged wire harness had slipped a bit on the last flight and she worried it would pull loose in midair, not a good thing.

"You want the rotor off?" the pilot asked her.

"Don't get nervous," she told him, grabbing her flashlight and screwdriver. The tech sergeant jumped from her seat and ran around the front of the helo, tucking her head down, though with her short frame she had plenty of clearance. The repaired wire harness sat in the housing next to the AN/ALQ-144A omnidirectional infrared jammer, which meant there was less than a foot—a lot less than a foot—of clearance between the cover and the whirling rotor blades. But Rosen wasn't attempting an overhaul; all she had to do was fight the damn tornado of wind and shine the flashlight in the right place. She threw herself against the side of Little Bird, toeing the rocket tube. Rosen grabbed the rear radio fin with her right hand and worked the flashlight with her left as she inched upward. She slid the screwdriver out along the flashlight with her thumb, then poked forward to nudge the metal back—she'd rigged the access panel for an easy view after the first flight, when her check cost them nearly fifteen minutes.

She leaned in to look. The thick electrical tape she'd wound around the harness to hold it was still solid. Rosen craned her neck just to check the front of the assembly when she felt her legs shifting out from under her. The Little Bird began to rise and move backward. She lost her grip and started to slide in the rush of wind. Her instinct was to hold the flashlight and the screwdriver, but something made her let go; she found herself falling, and at that moment her eyes went hard and her hands turned to claws. She grabbed for the rear door handle, kept falling. For a second she saw, she felt herself getting chewed up by the rear rotor, sliced and diced into dog food. Her soul fell into its secret niche; she fought to remove it, not ready for salvation, or at least not death. Rosen managed to kick her leg into the helo's body, then rolled her torso around to grab onto the rocket-launcher tube, landing half in and half out of the craft. She pushed herself into the back of the helicopter. Fernandez's horrified face loomed over hers.

"Okay," she shouted, getting up. "Okay, okay. Go. Go."

"Are you all right?"

"Go! Go!"

He waited until she had strapped herself in before pulling ahead.

The shadow of the Pave-Low in the distance told her what had happened—the draft from the bigger helicopter's massive whirly nearly knocked the Little Bird over.

"I'm sorry," Fernandez shouted back to her. "Christ, I'm sorry."

"No problem," she said. "Next time I'll wear my magnetic boots."

15

Major Horace "Hack" Preston scanned the F-15's instrument panel, moving quickly through the dials and indicators on the Eagle's high-tech dashboard. The large screen at
the top right was clean—no enemy radars were active, at
least not at the moment. He had plenty of fuel for the two
more turns they planned before going home; the rest of his
instruments declared the F-15C in showroom shape. Preston turned his gaze back to the HUD, which was projecting
its white lines, letters, and numbers in front of a steadily
darkening sky.

Their tour of Iraq had been extended as a result of some
last-minute tasking snafus. Hack had welcomed the double
shift, hoping it would give him a chance to redeem himself
for the botched chance earlier in the day. But now he was
just tired. Piranha One and Two were due to be relieved in

less than fifteen minutes; he'd go home eagerly and very possibly fall asleep before the debriefing ended.

He hadn't necessarily screwed up the MiG shot. On the contrary—he'd followed procedure to the letter, hesitating only because of the friendlies in the vicinity. He'd locked and launched within the Sparrow's optimum target range, then jinked his plane and launched countermeasures. Everything had been done precisely by the book.

But it nagged at him. He should have nailed the damn thing. Anything less was failure.

He acknowledged as his wingmate checked in with two more radar contacts. They ID'd the planes as F-111s en route to Baghdad.

"All quiet on the Western Front," added Johnny.

"Affirmative," he told his wingmate, expecting that the formal tone would discourage him from chitchat.

It did. The two Eagles continued their silent patrol of the skies, trekking along their racetrack at a leisurely four hundred and fifty nautical miles an hour. Fuel flowed steadily through their thirsty engines. The video screens and dashboard lights filled the cockpit with a soft glow. Hack worked methodically, fighting off fatigue, struggling to keep his focus as they completed their next-to-last circuit and headed north for one last run.

Somewhere far below, triple-A flared toward the heavens in a steady, thick stream of tracers. The gunfire was so furious that the line looked unbroken—a fairly sobering thought, given that typically only one in four of the rounds fired was a sparkler.

"Coming to our turn in zero-one minutes," Hack told his wingmate. They were in tactical separation, two miles abreast, with the wingman stacked above him about a thousand feet. The formation allowed each man to check the other's "six" or rear, and provided clearly defined hunting spheres for their missiles. Offsetting each other's altitude made it more difficult for an oncoming fighter pilot to spot both planes with one sweep of his eyes.

But the abreast formation did make turns a bit more difficult, especially in the dark; they had to be closely coordinated or the formation would be broken. The planes moved like parts in an old-fashioned clock. Hack called the turn and they went at it textbook style, Two pulling three g's as it started left, One easing around with a tight turn and rollout that picked up his wingmate precisely abeam, two miles apart, still stacked but heading south.

Twenty-five thousand feet, four hundred and sixty nautical miles an hour. F-111s passing ahead of them, twenty miles.

Hack got another contact below eight thousand feet about fifty miles to the east heading west. He tickled the identifier.

A-10A. The Warthogs were all over the place today.

"What do you figure that A-10 is doing this far north?" Hack asked his wingmate.

"Got me," said Johnny. "Maybe he's lost."

Hack debated asking the AWACS if it really was an A-10. Before he could decide, his radar kicked out three more low-level contacts, all moving relatively slow, farther southwest, most likely helos. He began to query them when the AWACS broke in with an alert.

"Two boogies coming off the deck," screeched the controller. "No three, four—damn, they're sending the whole air force after you."

16

Rosen, peering over Fernandez's shoulder, had just spotted Fort Apache in the distance when the AWACS called out the MiG warning. She sat back in the seat as the pilot leaned over and punched the controls for the radio.

"We'll monitor the interceptors," Fernandez explained. "We don't want them to see us at Apache but we have to make the pickup no matter what. We don't have enough fuel to screw around. If we stay low they may miss us."

"Yeah, yeah," she said. They had to get their guys out.

"There's our other Little Bird—you see it? He's just leaving the strip."

Fernandez needed both hands to control the helicopter, so he merely leaned his head forward. Rosen made out a low shadow ahead, darting across the left quarter of the windscreen. It was Apache Air One, the other Little Bird.

There would now be only two men left at the fort—Captain Hawkins and a gunner.

One of the fighter pilots squawked something about different targets and called a bearing number. It sounded to Rosen as if the Eagles were having difficulty locating the enemy planes, but she had never heard live air combat before. The voices had a clipped excitement to them, a high pitch that came through the static.

Fort Apache with its fatally short runway lay a few hundred yards ahead in the dust. Fernandez slowed the helicopter as he crossed over the concrete, looking to land near the ruins that had served as the base's command post.

Rosen thought of Lieutenant Dixon as she whipped off the com set and threw it into the front of the helo. His broken body lay somewhere to the north, unburied for all she knew, abandoned. She felt a cold blast of air from the open door, pulled her arms around her, and walled off the part of her mind where his memory lived, sealing it away permanently as a dangerous keepsake.

Parallel to the ruins, Fernandez tilted the back end of the craft up to spin around. Suddenly the control panel went dark and the AH-6 slammed against the ground.

"Shit!" said Fernandez, slamming his hand on the top of the panel as if the electrical short were there.

"It's the harness, it's the harness," yelled Rosen, jumping out of the craft. She pulled herself up to examine the panel before realizing she had lost her flashlight back at Sand Box when she'd slipped. She had to lean back and get Fernandez's light.

But her jury-rigged harness had held. What the hell?

It was difficult to see beyond the wires. She began to slide her hands along the harness but found them blocked by a jagged piece of metal. The metal moved when she moved her hand—it was part of the infrared jammer, which had come loose from the back of the motor assembly cover.

Not good.

Rosen slid her fingers around, gingerly touching the unit. The rotors were still winding down; it was hard to shine the light and hold on at the same time. She used her fingers to feel for the problem. They slid across wires and a narrow tube and metal. Finally, her pinkie slipped into an empty hole. Her forefinger found another and then a third.

"Turn everything off!" she yelped. "Off! Off!"

"It's off! It's dead! It's dead!" Fernandez yelled back, but by then Rosen had draped herself across the topside of the helo, craned between the rotor blades. Exactly one bolt, no thicker than a Bic pen, held the entire AN/ALQ-144A and its ceramic radiator in place. One of its flanges had severed several wires as the helicopter tipped to landing.

That was lucky. Had it flown off into the rotors, they would have gone straight down as fast as gravity could take them.

Rosen slipped down to the side of the helicopter and held the wire harness assembly aside. She pushed the jammer housing away about six inches before the bolt caught tight and refused to budge.

"Fuck you, Saddam!" she screamed, throwing her weight and fury headlong at the assembly, pushing it toward the side. The bolt hung on stubbornly, then sprang loose, sending her rolling headfirst across the cement. Parts of the ALQ-144 spewed around her as she fell.

Oblivious to what was happening, Hawkins and the other Delta trooper had been trotting nonchalantly toward the helicopter from a sandbagged position north of the landing strip, seemingly reluctant to leave. They saw Rosen fall and ran to her, yanking her up so fast that the blood that wasn't pouring from her scraped-up face rushed to her feet.

"Into the helicopter," she said, trying to shake them off. "Come on, come on. There are a bunch of Iraqi airplanes headed this way. We got to get out of here."

"Are you okay, Sergeant?" Hawkins asked.

"No," she said, grabbing the flashlight from the ground. She pulled the roll of black electrical tape from her pocket as she threw herself back onto the helicopter. The wires were all color-coded but she had no play; she had to yank the tape off her harness to get some. She pulled at the tape and then twisted the pairs together as quickly as she could, hoping her tape would hold.

She leaned down and yelled for Fernandez to see if he had power.

He did.

She had to add more tape to the front of the wire strands to make sure they'd stay put, now that they were exposed. The wind from the rotors threw sand into her eyes, but Rosen was operating in another universe now, one beyond the throb in her head and the screaming fire of her battered face. She punched the remaining shards of the jammer assembly base with her fist, bending or clearing away everything she could. Then she found a plastic wire clip flopping loose and managed to secure it against an exposed pin near the wires. Not pretty, certainly not permanent, but good enough.

"Go! Go! Go!" she yelped, flinging herself back into the back cabin feet first. "Why the hell aren't you going!"

"We *are* going," shouted Fernandez, emphasizing his point by slamming the helo forward, full throttle.

17

Doberman acknowledged the AWACS snap vector with a grumble, putting the Hog into the directed turn at nearly a right angle.

Not that he resented the E-3 Sentry and its powerful airborne radar. What really irked him was that he had to climb to fifteen thousand feet, per standing orders, as he approached the Saudi border. Granted, the altitude kept him safe from triple-A nasties, but it was a piss-poor place to be with a flock of MiGs coming for you. Besides, the Hog didn't *like* flying this high, and neither did he.

Fifty feet above ground level, dark be damned. That was where he belonged.

Doberman got his Hog on the new course east, then dialed into the intercept, listening as the interceptors began to break down the approaching enemy flight. Unlike most

Iraqi scrambles, this one seemed intent on actually doing something—the bandits, definitely identified now as MiG-29s, weren't running away.

Doberman tacked their courses on the blackboard of his mind. They were north and west of him, heading in the general direction of Fort Apache.

His RWR screamed something, and the AWACS controller yelped another warning. A ground-control radar for a high-altitude SA-2 had turned itself on directly ahead on the AWACS directed course.

Doberman cursed and threw his plane into a fresh maneuver, beaming the radar by temporarily heading north. The radar went off as quickly as it had come on. He judged that he was already outside the range of the missiles but there was no sense taking chances; he took the plane three miles north before pulling around to the southwest.

As he did, the AWACS announced that it had discovered a MiG-21 Fishbed flying under cover of the larger MiG-29s. The plotted course had it headed straight for him, and now the controller rattled Doberman's helmet with a warning that it was juicing its afterburners.

That was the last straw. He kicked the Hog over into a full dive, gunning down to where the air was thick and the ground effects heavy. If the Iraqi kept coming, good. Doberman had snapped his last vector tonight.

Let the bastard come and get him. They'd slug it out, mud fighter to mud fighter, if the Iraqi had the balls to take on a Hog.

18

This time, Hack wasn't going to miss. He twisted his Eagle northward for the intercept, ignoring the pinch and pull of gravity as he snapped onto the vector supplied by the AWACS. His radar screen laid out the bandits as if peering down from above. The hostile MiGs were at the very top, triangles with pointers coming off their noses to show their headings. The screen flagged friendlies as circles with similar pointers, along with way markers for reference.

The radio exploded with a cacophony of calls and commands, a chaotic wail that had confused him during the earlier encounter. But this time Hack was prepared—he and his wingman keyed into a clear frequency they had surveyed earlier.

"Two bandits, ten o'clock, your zone," said Johnny, his voice crisp.

"Out of range. Two more coming behind them," Hack said.

"Something low."

There were now six triangles very close together on the screen. Two veered to the left and temporarily disappeared, possibly obscured by the reflected ground clutter. The other four Iraqi planes altered course, vectoring toward the flight of F-111s.

Hack rechecked the IDs, making sure he had the unfriendlies.

No answer. The lead contact was thirty miles away.

"First two are mine," he told Johnny. The radar and its weapons-control computer had already locked them up. They were tagged on the HUD; he could launch and take them out at will. "You got the others?"

"Negative, negative. I'm having some trouble here."

"Johnny?"

"Uh, okay, I have it. I—shit, I'm spiked."

The lead MiG had just turned its radar on his wingmate. Time to pull the trigger.

"Fox One, Fox One! I'm on number two. Firing. Fox One!"

Hack yelled so loud his wingmate probably could have heard him without a radio. He didn't bother jinking or trying to beam the enemy radars—if his wingmate couldn't target the other interceptors, he was going to have to close and take them out with his Sidewinders.

The four enemy planes—still out of visual range but closing quickly—began moving wildly on his radar screen. One of his missiles seemed to hit—the lead plane, he thought—but now everything was moving so quickly that Hack couldn't afford to divide his attention long enough to make sure he'd gotten the kill. Something beamed him dead ahead. He thumbed into auto-guns mode, then realized he'd dropped to sixteen thousand feet and was still pointing downward. He began to pull back on the stick when a dark shape shot in front of him, less than a mile away.

His stomach flared as he waited for the glare of a missile or cannon tracer. He pushed the Eagle over on her wing, desperate to duck away. He got a warning, a second warning—sounds and buzzes and lights, and once more his head was swimming with sweat, gravity, and panic.

Gravity pushing against his chest, Hack realized the shadow had been one of the F-111s, not a MiG. He cursed himself, rolled level, tried to raise his wingmate on the radio. The small circle representing Piranha Two floated across the HUD, but Hack had lost track of where he was.

Fear twinged at the corner of his stomach.

Not this time, he told himself. *Clear your head. Do your best.*

Something exploded about three hundred yards in front of his right wing. Fire flew through the air.

The pipper had a triangle boxed at ten o'clock. He leaned on his trigger, getting off a quick shot but missing as the enemy wagged away. He saw the red circle growing oblong and started to follow, thumbed a Sidewinder online, but he was too slow and had misjudged the enemy's turn in the dark. For a second he was in deep shit—inside and ahead of the MiG, the worst place to be. But somehow, knowing exactly where he was cleared his head. Somehow, his stomach went hard and his eyes became focused, and he gave the big Eagle more thrust than a Saturn V heading for the moon. The plane shot forward, twisting out of danger as he spit out chaff and flares.

And then it was over.

The cockpit went silent. The night became black. Hack heard his breath loud in his ears, saw that he was level at fifteen thousand feet.

Carefully, almost slowly, he got his bearings and did his instrument checks, pointing the nose of the Eagle southward.

"Piranha One, this is Two," said Johnny. "I'm lost airman."

"Yeah, okay, okay, okay." The words slurred out of his mouth; he couldn't stop them or change them into anything coherent. But that was all right—his head was clear, and he calmly found his wingmate only two miles to the northeast, though well higher than him. Johnny began turning and Hack continued his climb, heart steady and almost slow.

"I think I nailed one of those MiGs," he told his wingman.

"I think you nailed two."

"Yeah?" Hack started to ask whether he'd seen the explosions when he got a new contact on his radar. It was running south at four thousand feet, about two miles west of where the MiG had snuck in and almost unzipped him.

"We have a fresh contact, Piranha Two," he said, changing course to catch it.

19

The MiG-21 changed course twice as Doberman pitched downward, adjusting to his zigs with ominous zags of its own. Knowing he couldn't lose the MiG's Jay Bird radar until he was under three thousand feet, Doberman poured on the gas, hurtling down so fast he worried about tearing the plane's wings off.

The MiG-21 was a rugged and quick interceptor, well suited to aerial combat. It was fast, maneuverable, and small. While its avionics systems were not comparable to frontline fighters like the F-15 or even the F-16, it out-classed the A-10A as a dogfighter by miles. It was capable of carrying beyond-visual-range weapons and could even be fitted with infrared night-vision equipment, advantages Doberman couldn't hope to counter in a dogfight. His best bet was scrambling around in the ground clutter until the Iraqi lost interest or the Eagles chased him off.

As Doberman's altitude dipped below 2,500 feet, he pulled the Hog into a tight turn north, slashing around in a twisting roll that pulled nearly five g's, in theory more than the plane's rated capacity. He began pushing the stick to level off before realizing the horizon bar showed him heading straight downward. The wings started yawing on him and he had a fight now; he was behind the plane, temporarily out of control, reacting to it instead of having it react to him. He got angry—he screamed at the plane to cut the bullshit—and as gravity tore at his face and chest, he managed to steady the wings and back off on his speed, pulling out in something approaching a controlled glide. He leveled off at three hundred feet, a lot lower than he wanted to be. The MiG was still up there somewhere, but he didn't have any indication of it on his gear. The sky above and ahead was a uniform gray. He twisted his neck back and forth, trying to make sure his six was clear as he got his nose pointed directly south.

Doberman felt a cold stream of sweat running down the side of his flightsuit as he stared through his front windscreen. He put his hand on the throttle, pegging his speed at three hundred and fifty knots. He didn't like not knowing where the enemy was. He tried hailing the AWACS but didn't get a response.

The MiG might have passed by him already. In that case, it would be turning around somewhere ahead.

Or not. He was still deep inside Iraq. He started working out his position with the help of his paper map when he saw a stubby building break the undulating ground ahead; he saw a long, straight line and realized he was heading over

Fort Apache's landing strip. His brain seemed to contract—he hadn't realized he'd come this far east, let alone this far north.

Doberman nudged his nose up, working to give himself a little more breathing room while staying in the ground clutter.

A sand dune moved to the right.

No, a plane.

He jumped back in his seat, his mind computing the scenario as his eyes and ears threw the flight data at it.

MiG, closing for a front-quarter cannon attack. Kill him head-on.

No, it wanted him to break; he'd close on Doberman and use his heat-seekers.

RWR. He was spiked.

No, nothing. But obviously it saw him; it was coming for him.

Turning was suicidal. But if Doberman didn't break, the MiG would go around, use his superior speed to catch him.

Nail him as he came through. Snapshot by yanking into him.

A millisecond of opportunity.

Then what? Where would he be?

The MiG would come at him from the offset, angling, cheating so he could cut into a tight merge, slide into his victim's tail no matter what he did.

The Hog could outturn the MiG. The Iraqi wouldn't expect that—the Fishbed could knife around anything else in the sky. If Doberman could brave the front-quarter attack, he could turn inside him, twist back down and away.

Better—let him get on his back but with his nose out,

then turn inside quickly, at the first moment, have him go past. A tangled rope.

Nail him with the Sidewinders on the Hog's right wing.

Show the son of a bitch not to mess with Hogs.

Turn the damn things on. The seeker heads have to do some calisthenics to warm up—or rather cool down, so the head can pick up the SOB's heat.

Where is my goddamn radar and the RWR and the AWACS and those stinking Eagles?

Hell, ask for AMRAAMs while you're at it.

Doberman snorted, laughing at himself. He pushed the nose of his plane toward the approaching hulk, heart pounding, ready to take his shot.

Then he realized it wasn't a MiG.

He nudged his stick back; he was coming at the tail end of a helicopter, closing so fast the helo seemed to be standing still.

An American bird, running dark—one of the Spec Ops AH-6s. He glanced at his kneepad for their radio frequency when the RWR screamed that the MiG was closing from above for the kill.

20

Sitting in the backseat of the helicopter, Rosen had a difficult time puzzling out the situation from what the others were saying. There were apparently two different sets of Iraqi planes nearby, possibly coming for them. One of the groups included at least two MiG-29s; these were being engaged by F-15s.

The other was a single plane, probably a MiG-21. It was somewhere right behind them.

There was also an A-10A around somewhere—Devil One, Captain Glenon. The Hog had descended rapidly to their north; it wasn't clear whether it was trying to hide in the ground effects that confused radar or if it had been hit.

For years, Rosen had listened to accounts of dogfights that seemed like clear-cut maneuvers—two fighters approached each other, one saw the other first, missiles were launched, bad guys smashed. But the reality of an honest-to-God furball defied description. It was like running through a swirling pile of leaves with your eyes closed, trying to grab a dollar bill. Even the best sensors could only show you two dimensions of reality.

"MiG closing off our port side," snapped the pilot. "Eight o'clock. He's at five thousand feet, diving on us. If he hasn't spotted us already, he will in a second."

Rosen took that to mean she ought to grab on to something and hold tight.

21

The contact was low, below a thousand feet. Another plane was approaching from the north and there was a helo or something else incredibly slow in front.

Nobody answered IDs. Hack guessed that the helo was a Coalition Spec Ops craft; they'd been briefed during pre-flight to watch for operations here. The two contacts going in its direction must be Iraqis trying to nail it.

He lost the lead aircraft momentarily. The second one, gaining, had been tentatively ID'd as a MiG by the AWACS.

The first plane popped back up on the screen, closing on the helicopter. Hack was still fifteen miles away, too far to launch the Sidewinders. He tickled the IDs again.

Nada.

RWR was clear. The enemy planes didn't realize he was here.

Ten miles. If he'd had any more Sparrows left, the bastards would be dead.

Sidewinders would nail them, soon as he closed. AIM-9s were ready and waiting.

The lead plane was going to nail the helo any second. He was already in range.

Hack corrected as the planes began dancing wildly; he had to keep his target within a 45 degree aiming cone to ensure the kill.

Eight miles, seven.

Nada.

Lead bandit's going to nail the helo.

The second plane, the one ID'd as a MiG, had the stops out.

He couldn't get them both in one swoop. Stay on the leader.

Five miles. The first plane jinked suddenly, pushing out of the optimum firing cone. Hack moved his stick to follow, waited for the growl from the Sidewinder telling him he had a hot target. His radar coughed up an unidentified contact dead west, flying north very low. He started to run through his queries one more time, still waiting for the Sidewinder to lock.

As it did, the IFF in the lead bandit beamed back a signal to Hack's Eagle.

The plane closing on the helicopter was an A-10.

Oh my God, Hack thought, jerking his finger away from the trigger. *I almost nailed a good guy.*

22

The ancient ALQ-119 ECM pod on Doberman's right wing cranked away, filling the airwaves with a cacophonous symphony of electronic confusion. Designed to drive 60's-era radars and every dog within a hundred miles nuts, the Westinghouse unit was a first-generation noise-and-deception jammer that had joined the service before Doberman had. In theory, it was obsolete and of little value here.

But either it was working or the MiG pilot was doing a very convincing impression of being blind, for the Fishbed streaked down nearly in front of him, seemingly unaware that Doberman was now right on his tail. Doberman didn't even have to move his stick as the low growl sounding from the Sidewinder AIM-9L indicated it had acquired its target.

Something about the way the shape fluctuated in his windshield made Doberman hesitate; in the next second the

MiG flashed downward and to the right. He lost his firing position, had to pull the Hog tight over his shoulder to get the front of the plane back onto its target. He saw the helo out of the corner of his eye but couldn't find the MiG, sensed it had turned around him, trying for a shooting angle.

Now he was the quarry.

Doberman worked the Hog tighter, climbing slightly then pushing the nose back down, bucking the plane in midair and swirling around. He heard another growl but worried the Sidewinder had locked on the helicopter. It took only a millisecond to realize it hadn't, but by then he'd lost the shot again, the MiG cranking and wanking in a series of high-g turns that Doberman couldn't keep up with. He pulled his wings level, eyes blurry. He tried focusing on the compass heading, unsure where the hell he'd spun himself around to, when a sudden shudder passed over the Hog. The MiG had cleared his right wing at less than ten feet.

It was going south. With nothing between it and the Fort Apache helicopter.

"Damn me," he yelled, and this time he yanked the stick so hard the only thing that kept it tied into its boot was the massive smack of gravity that punched the plane in the face. There was a theory that the Hog couldn't withstand anything higher than three g's, but no Hog driver had ever subscribed to that notion, and if Doberman had been able to talk, he would have sworn twenty g's grabbed him and his airplane as it changed direction.

Amazingly, the wings stayed on the aircraft. So did the engines, which had every right to flame out but kept spinning just the same. Doberman found the tail of the MiG disappearing into a mist of sand a quarter mile ahead. He'd almost pushed the button to fire the AIM-9s when he realized he wasn't locked. He jiggled the Hog to the right, hoping somehow that realigning his nose would give him a better target. It didn't; he saw something below him on the desert floor, a small lump—the helo had stopped.

He caught a glimpse of it, saw that it was intact, whirlies whirling. He got his eyes back to where they belonged, couldn't find the MiG, realized he'd flown to barely twenty feet. If he didn't start climbing soon, he was going to become part of the landscape.

Doberman pulled back on the stick, easing upward. He got to eight hundred feet when he realized where the MiG was.

He yanked the Hog's left wing over just in time to avoid the rush of a close-quarter cannon over his canopy, but didn't have enough altitude to chance more than a shallow roll before recovering. A fresh stream of cannon exploded in front of his canopy and he felt something nudge his wing, an angel tapping him to see if he was ready for heaven.

The MiG had hung with him somehow and was right on his back. The stream of its tracers jerked toward his canopy.

Then the front of his cockpit filled with a dark green shadow. Thunder and lightning roiled around him and the air reverberated with exploding brimstone.

"Hog Rule number one!" shouted a familiar voice in his earphones. "Never leave home without your wingman!"

Captain Thomas "Shotgun" O'Rourke had arrived.

23

Shotgun's front-quarter attack was mostly flash—heads-on was a notoriously difficult way to shoot down an enemy, even when you could see what you were doing—but it had the desired effect. The MiG broke off, banking hard to Shotgun's left as they passed.

"I got him low," Shotgun told Doberman as he began pulling the Hog around so the MiG couldn't get him from behind. "He's west of us, west. Shit, I've lost him."

Shotgun had a real hunger for some Good & Plenty, but the little pellets of licorice had a nasty habit of sliding down your mouth in the middle of a high-g turn. He decided to settle for a Tootsie Roll. He had just reached for one when instinct told him his six was hot—he shoved his Hog down and to the left, ducking a nasty round of cannon fire from the MiG's GSh-23.

Okay, so the Iraqi pilot's pretty good, Shotgun thought as the Fishbed tried to hang with him on the turn. The MiG had to slow down to make the maneuver, and Shotgun tried taking advantage of his tighter turning radius by breaking away to the south. But the MiG pilot managed to stay with him, crossing back as they yo-yoed through the night sky. A fresh round of shells sliced just over the Hog's fuselage.

Shotgun cranked hard again back to the right. If he could let the MiG go ahead, he'd fire the Sidewinders up its tailpipe. But the Iraqi had realized the Hog could turn inside him; he stayed back, letting Shotgun cut his tight zigs and then using his bigger engine to catch up. Shotgun saw what the Iraqi was doing as a fresh set of tracers flared at an angle past his windshield. He bucked the Hog low and tried a full circle. The MiG stayed right with him, occasionally winking its GSh in his direction.

With an afterburner, the Hog would have easily snapped away and been gone. But Shotgun didn't have the horses to outrun the Iraqi, or even to break the twisting yo-yo. He cut left, then right, and got some fresh tracers across his wings.

Only one thing to do—crank up the Boss and wait for Doberman to nail him.

Good thing he'd had the foresight to put on *The River* before setting sail north. This might take a while.

24

All of thirty seconds had passed since Shotgun had chased
the MiG from his tail, but to Doberman it felt like a month.
He broke left as the MiG broke right, clearing the Iraqi and
the swirling chaos that had wrapped itself around his head.
Banking to the north, trying to sort out the situation, he saw
the dark shadow of the AH-6 picking itself up off the
ground.

There were two F-15 Eagles somewhere above. Another
four were rushing north. The MiG was either extremely
lucky or flying too low for them to get a good fix. Shotgun,
after his initial radio yahoo, had gone silent and, for the moment at least, disappeared. All Doberman could hear over
the radio was a loud hushing roar—something like the
sound of a freight train out of control.

Doberman felt his anxiety growing as he hunted for his

wingman. Be just like Shotgun to get nailed saving his—Doberman's—butt.

Shotgun? Nailed?

Yeah, right. Hostess would stop making cupcakes before that happened.

An oblong blue flame caught Doberman's attention as he began pushing his Hog's nose south. He squeezed the throttle for its last ounce of thrust; two dark specks twisted against the ground a mile and a half in front of him. Tracers lit the night; the second plane had a commanding position on the first plane's tail, but the lead pilot refused to give in, somehow knowing exactly where his enemy was going to fire before he did. The planes swirled to the south.

No way in the world Shotgun would have missed at that range. He must be the one in the lead.

Doberman pushed the stick right then slammed it left, dead-on the tail of the MiG, four miles behind it.

Something screamed—it was the AIM-9Ls, begging him to fire already.

He squeezed off, felt the swish, keyed his mike to sound the warning that the missile was away.

"Fox Two! Fox Two!"

Before he got the words out of his mouth, the MiG exploded.

EPILOGUE

SOME OTHER PLAYER

1

Doberman's legs began shaking as he lifted himself over the side of the Hog. Cold, tired, hungry, barely alive—but the thing that was getting to him, had got to him, was Becky Rosen standing on the access ramp, waiting to congratulate him. About a dozen people, including Shotgun and Tinman and a parcel of Delta troopers, stood behind her, but all he saw was her. Somehow, he got down the ladder without falling.

"Hey," he said, finally getting his feet firmly on the ground.

She jumped on him and he fell back against the ladder. She kissed him on the cheek and his face flushed. The others swarmed in, pumping him on the back and the shoulder and the head, whatever they could touch.

As far as anyone knew, Captain John "Doberman"

Glenon had scored the first ever shootdown of a MiG in the slow and lumbering A-10A.

"It's what I'm talking about!" Shotgun declared, more or less summarizing everyone's sentiments.

Everything hit Doberman at once—the long day and night of missions they'd endured before the forced landing at Apache, the retank, Al-Kajuk, the dogfight. Doberman squeezed Rosen hard then laughed and found Shotgun in the press of people right in front of him.

"You saved my life," he told him. He threw his arms around his wingman—not an easy task. "You saved my goddamned life. That MiG almost nailed me."

"Ah, you would have gotten away from him sooner or later," Shotgun said. "Sorry it took me so long to get off the ground here. Tinman had to hunt for spare parts or something. I wasn't even across the border when the AWACS told me you'd just sent the Pave Hawk home. I figured you'd head over to Apache."

"I don't know how I ended up there," admitted Doberman. "I was ducking a SAM site and some MiGs. I swear to God, I just looked down and there was Apache. No shit. I thought I was about fifty miles closer to the border."

"Lucky for us you got lost," said Rosen. "You saved us."

"Damn straight," yelled Hawkins, the Spec Ops captain from Fort Apache. Everybody started yelling and touching him for good luck again.

Finally, Doberman managed to slide free. He walked over to the end of the wing where the double rail of Sidewinders sat—now with only a single AIM-9L.

"I got it," he said. "Shit. I got it."

*   *   *

Two or three hours later a grim-faced Air Force officer wearing a fairly crisp uniform and the gold oak leaf of a major found Doberman sitting alone against a set of sandbags not far from the A-10A service area Rosen and her team of techies had dubbed Oz West. Doberman had slipped away from the others, intending at first to go to sleep, but he was too pumped for that. He'd ended up sitting and staring at the plane in the dark. At first he thought about the mission. Then he started thinking about Dixon, the Hog driver who'd died up north working as a spotter with the Delta team. Kid reminded him a lot of his little brother.

"Captain Glenon?" asked the major, who'd flown there from Riyadh. "I'd like to speak to you."

Doberman lifted his eyes slowly, focusing on the man in the dim light reflected from the work area. He could guess that the major was here to debrief him. He'd already spoken to two intel officers, though admittedly their interviews had barely covered the bones of what had happened. There was much more information to be gleaned; Black Hole and the Central Command would be especially interested in the Scuds and the mosque.

But Doberman felt too drained for it all.

"Do you mind if we do this in the morning?" Doberman asked him. "I'm a little tired."

"This isn't something that can wait," said the major stiffly. "And I'm afraid you're not going to like it."

Doberman listened as the officer told him, succinctly, without emotion or digression, that he would not be given credit for the air-to-air kill. Fort Apache and the rest of the Delta missions north had to remain a closely guarded secret. That included the airplanes that had assisted them, and their missions.

"Officially, you're still at King Fahd," the lieutenant major told him. "You never shot down a MiG; the kill will be credited to another unit. I'm sorry, I know it must feel like a punch in the gut, but it's to save other people's lives. I know that's important to you, Captain."

Doberman pulled himself to his feet.

"Captain? Are you all right?"

Doberman shrugged. He honestly didn't care about getting credit.

Poor Dixon. The kid had been a great stick-and-rudder man, a real talent—raw and inexperienced, naive, but damn good. On the ground, though, he was just so much fodder.

Central Command probably had him listed as being back at King Fahd, too.

"Captain?" asked the man from Riyadh.

"I'm just a little tired right now," Doberman told him, finally feeling like he could fall asleep. "Whatever you guys want to do, that's fine with me."

2

Final credit would have to wait for an exhaustive review of
the tapes and AWACS data, but the rest of Piranha
Squadron welcomed Major Horace Preston as a conquering
hero. They'd already gotten verbal confirmation from the
AWACS controller that both of his Sparrows had nailed
their targets.

He'd also come close to downing the first A-10 of the
war, a fact he made clear as he and Johnny debriefed the
mission. If the Warthogs were going to go so far north, they
sure as hell better have their IFFs working properly. It had
been just a freak thing that he got the ID before firing the
Sidewinder.

"AWACS tried calling you," Johnny told him when they
were alone. "They had the A-10 ID'd."

Hack bristled. He'd been surprised to find all four radar

missiles on his wingmate's wings when he returned. He had shrugged noncommittally at the pilot's explanation that he couldn't lock up his targets; it was certainly possible that there had been some sort of mechanical screwup. But he planned on checking on it himself in the morning.

"The A-10 was still pretty lucky," said Hack.

"Definitely. Still, guy must be a pretty good pilot," said Johnny. "To nail a MiG with a Sidewinder."

"Yeah," said Hack grudgingly. Undoubtedly the shoot-down had been due to luck, not skill. But he was too tired now to argue.

The Warthogs didn't belong north of the border without heavy escort; he'd make that clear to the general when he talked to him tomorrow.

On the other hand, maybe he shouldn't bring that up. The way his luck was running, he'd get stuck baby-sitting them.

A few hours later Hack was woken from a fitful sleep by a sergeant who told him he had an important phone call. The sergeant claimed not to know who it was, which led Hack to guess it was an Air Force public-relations liaison. He'd seen other guys interviewed after successful dogfights; now it was his turn.

He pulled on his boots and dressed quickly, shaking his head to wake up. The brass in D.C. would undoubtedly be listening in. This was definitely a career builder, a chance that wouldn't come again.

The squadron commander met him at the door to his office.

"Come on, Hack. Don't want to keep the general waiting too long."

"General on the phone? Who?"

The squadron leader smiled, as if that were answer enough. Hack slipped down into his boss's well-padded leather chair and held the receiver to his ear.

"Hack? This is Bobby Sherman. Congratulations."

"Thanks, General. Thank you very much," he said. Sherman, a two-star general with the Tactical Air Command back in the States, was one of several people who had mentored him through the ranks. It was flattering that he had called—still, it was a bit of a letdown. Hack had been hoping he would be on the *Today* show, or at least CNN. "It wasn't that much, really. It happened so fast."

"So fast? What are you talking about?" the general asked.

Hack straightened in the chair. "The shootdown, sir? The two MiGs."

"Hack, you son of a bitch—you splashed two MiGs?"

"They're, uh, not confirmed yet, sir." He was confused—why had the general called?

"That's fantastic. Well, listen, I have news for you—you're now DO of the 535th Tactical Fighter Squadron. Which actually sets you up very nicely to become its new commander, especially with those MiGs to your credit."

"Excuse me, General?"

"The papers are on their way. You're to report ASAP. I knew you'd want to know. This is the big one, Hack. The 535th is technically a wing—you'll be a wing commander as soon as it's brought up to strength. I would expect things to fall in place very, very quickly."

DO wasn't exactly what he had in mind. At best, the director of operations was the second in command—the guy with all the crap work to do. And the 535th? Whose unit was that?

"Hack?"

"The 535th is an F-16 squadron?" he asked.

"No. A-10s. The word is, the CO's on the way out. He's a washed-up old alchy past due for retirement. He's got a few friends here and there, but they won't be able to cover his ass much longer."

Hack tried to think of a way to refuse the assignment gracefully. No position with an A-10 squadron, not even commander, was acceptable.

Warthogs! Shit.

"I didn't realize you had so many hours in the Warthog cockpit until I went through your file," added Sherman. "That made it simple. I could have done this last year if I'd known. Hack, you with me?"

"I, uh, I . . ." There was no way to be diplomatic about it. "I'd like to stay with F-15s," he blurted.

"This is your career we're talking about," snapped the general. Hack could practically feel the fire.

"I, uh—"

"I woke you up, didn't I?" said the general, sliding back into his good-ol'-boy voice.

"Yes, sir."

"Well, go back to bed. Relax. You'll be heading that wing in no time. Commander's a guy named Michael Knowlington. You know him?"

"Oh shit," said Hack, every muscle in his body sagging.

"Hack?"

"Yes, sir, I do."

"Stay on his butt and you'll be commander and full colonel in a month."

Hack slid the phone back onto the cradle without saying anything else.

3

Skull had already talked to Rosen as well as the Special Operations command, so he had a pretty good handle on the official line—which, as he could easily have guessed, was that Fort Apache didn't exist. Therefore, the airdrop of an unauthorized female tech sergeant behind enemy lines had never taken place. Still, he felt some trepidation when he stepped into his office to take the call from his commanding general. He would not lie, but he would also not volunteer information, at least until he had a good feel for what the general knew—and, more importantly, felt—about the matter.

That would take several phone calls, all of which would have to wait for morning. He steeled himself to answer direct questions directly as he picked up the receiver and leaned back in his austere office chair.

But the general hadn't called to talk about Rosen.

"Mikey, I have news for you that will stick in your craw, but you're going to have to deal with it," declared the general.

"What's that?" Skull said. Few people had earned the right to call him Mikey; the general, with whom he'd never flown, wasn't one of them.

"A new DO has been assigned to your squadron."

He drew a breath. Bringing another officer into the squadron command structure was hardly unheard of, and given that Devil Squadron currently had no pilot above captain's rank on its rolls, Skull had thought the matter might be broached. But this had a very dangerous smell to it.

"I had been led to believe that I was to choose from my own men," he told the general. "I have several candidates. And if I can go outside the squadron—"

"No, Mikey, this isn't a debate thing. Major Preston will join you in the morning."

"Preston?"

"Horace Preston. I can't go into the politics; it's just happening."

"Thanks for the heads-up," said Skull. He put the receiver down.

The colonel knew Major Horace Gordon Preston well. During Skull's last stint at the Pentagon, Preston had tried to get him canned for incompetence and alcoholism.

Knowlington sat at the desk for nearly an hour. He didn't replay old missions or recite a Twelve Step mantra. He didn't think about the young pilot he'd lost, or the other men, or the friends. He didn't think about the dark cloud that sank around your head when things moved too fast and you lost yourself in the furball, or the way your stomach disappeared when gravity pushed too hard, or how your whole body squeezed into a narrow heartbeat when the enemy had you fat in his targeting screen. He didn't think about the hopelessness of watching a friend get nailed, or the sick, hollow sound in your head when you heard that a man you'd sent up wasn't coming back. He tried not to think about the burning sensation on your tongue that followed the first sip of whiskey, or the electricity in your throat.

He stared at the blank wall. He stared until finally there was a knock on the door.

"Come," he said, his eyes still pasted on the wall.

"Colonel Knowlington," said Captain Bristol Wong, pushing open the door. "Sir, I need a word."

Knowlington turned and signaled with his hand that he should come in and sit down. Wong closed the door with one of his slow-handed gestures, shuffling his feet more than normal.

"You're up late," Skull told the captain.

Wong nodded. "I have to make a report," he said. "I expect that portions, when officially prepared, will be code-worded."

Knowlington waited. It was almost impossible to tell when Wong was being serious and when he was making some sort of sly, obscure joke.

He seemed to be doing both.

"I assume that by now you know that I was sent into Iraq," continued Wong. "I assure you that I was ordered to accompany Technical Sergeant Rosen against my wishes, and only after fully reminding the commanding officer of the implications of his order. Nonetheless, given the extreme circumstances, I judged it a lawful order and there-fore—"

"Don't worry about it, Wong. Officially, it never hap-pened."

The captain nodded. "I expected as much. While in Iraq, I obtained information that appeared to indicate the pres-ence of chemical-warhead material associated with known Scud capabilities. I accompanied a fire team to assess the situation. The SS-1s were apparently destroyed, though at present we lack information regarding the content of the warheads. Regardless of what those warheads contained, we cannot rule out the possession of them at the mosque ap-parently used as a depot."

Knowlington nodded. He'd heard about the mosque from the Delta commander.

"I will suggest that further investigation be undertaken," said Wong.

"I'm sure Black Hole's on it," said Knowlington.

"U-2 and satellite surveillance will be insufficient."

Knowlington sighed. "If you're looking for me to lobby somebody for Delta Force and another commando raid, I have to tell you—I helped plan the Apache mission only under orders. I was against sending Hogs that far north, let alone basing them there. What's with you, Wong? You told me the other day that going after the Scuds was a waste of manpower."

"There are two additional factors, sir." Wong's head bobbed up and down like a dashboard Buddha. "While I was north, I had some extended interaction with a special unit of Iraqis."

"What do you mean, interaction? Use English."

"I was captured and held for a brief period of time by a

small unit of non-Islamic Iraqis. They were obviously not part of the security unit guarding the Scuds and had access to considerable firepower."

"You were captured?"

"It is irrelevant," said Wong. "Except that it allowed me to obtain this."

The captain unfolded two sheets of notebook paper.

"This Arabic?" Knowlington asked.

"It is actually a code in Arabic," said Wong. "It says, 'Straw midnight, January 26th.'"

"You know, the problem here, Captain, is that I can never tell when you're fooling around."

Wong drew himself upright in the chair, his cheeks puffing and then deflating as he drew a long breath.

"I assure you, Colonel," he said. "I am not fooling around. The unit that detained me was obviously a Special Forces group, exactly the type employed as presidential bodyguards. I believe that 'Straw' is Saddam, and that he will visit Al-Kajuk in twenty-four hours, if my watch is operating properly."

"Saddam?"

Wong said nothing else. Knowlington pushed his fingers together, resting them on his taut stomach. It seemed a wild supposition, and coming from anyone else, Skull would never have believed it. Wong, though—that was something else.

"This isn't one of your jokes?"

"Sir, I have never been so serious about something in my life."

The colonel nodded. "I assume this will be in your reports."

"Of course."

"Well, it's out of our hands, then," he told him, standing. "Fort Apache's shut down, and our squadron's going back to tank plinking near the border. Which, I don't mind saying, is where our planes belong."

Wong remained seated. "There's one additional item you will want to hear, and which won't appear in any of the reports," he said. "I believe that Lieutenant Dixon is alive, or at least he was this afternoon."

"What?"

"Someone fired an AK-47 at the Iraqis," Wong explained. "It was not a member of the Delta fire team, and could not have been an Iraqi. But there was definitely some other player involved, and he almost surely saved my life."

"Another player meaning who?"

"As far as I have been able to ascertain, no Coalition team, American or British SAS, was within twenty miles of Al-Kajuk at the time. But the quarry where Lieutenant Dixon was last seen lies within an easy hike."

"Dixon's dead, Captain. He was seen lying on the ground in the quarry right before it was hit."

"Perhaps," said Wong. "But I believe he's alive. It is the only explanation that makes sense to me. I truly believe it was him."

"If you're right," said Skull, "we're going to have to go back and get him."

"I'm sure I'm right, sir."

"Then you better go get some sleep. Tomorrow's going to be a very long day."

A Note to Readers

While I hope I've told this tale in a way that allows new readers to join right in, *Snake Eaters* picks up where *Fort Apache* left off; I hope you'll go back and read that book—number three in the series—when you get a chance. Of course, I hope you'll read the others as well.

While based on actual events and missions in the Gulf War, this is a work of fiction and should be treated as such. Some things are more fictional than others. Technical Sergeant Rosen, for example, would never have been sent north of the border in real life. That would be totally against military regulations and procedure, which are always strictly followed, especially in war.

Fiction can't adequately portray the true courage and abilities of the many women who did go across the border under circumstances every bit as daunting as those faced by the good sergeant. Among them was Major Rhonda Cornum, who recounts her experience of being captured in *The Rhonda Cornum Story,* published by Presidio Press. You might check it out.

As this story was being written, American A-10As and

F 15s were once more in action over Europe and in the Gulf. In some minor instances, I thought it prudent to gloss over or omit some technical details of operations and equipment. In no case did that affect the story—though I was tempted, I have to admit, to give Doberman's Hog uprated engines toward the end.